Bree's _____ er and tighter as she _____ e possibility that she might actually be pregnant. It would certainly explain the nausea. But so could a lot of other things.

All she could do right now was hope for the best. And plan for the worst.

She grabbed a test, threw it into the basket and made her way to the front of the store. The person at the register was done so the guy in front of her moved forward, putting the things from his basket on the conveyor belt, glancing back at her.

Oh, no!

No, no, NO! The words screamed through her head.

Diego stood there, a smile coming to his face when he saw her. "Hi. Getting something for dinner tonight?"

Her tongue stuck to the roof of her mouth and no amount of trying would get it to budge. He glanced at her basket and stood there as his items slowly traveled away from him on the conveyor belt. For a minute no one moved.

Then his eyes slowly met hers.

Dear Reader,

People say to never make life decisions when going through a major crisis. But what if you did? What if someone you trusted deeply betrayed you, and you never got the chance to confront them?

That is what Bree Frost is faced with after the death of her fiancé on her wedding day. As she discovers things about him that he'd hidden, she finds solace in a one-night stand, only to discover the man she slept with is someone with whom she'll be working closely. Worse, she finds herself in a situation she never dreamed of.

But sometimes you find happiness in unexpected places. In unexpected events. Thank you for joining Bree and heart surgeon Diego Pintor on the beautiful island of Sicily as they struggle to put the painful pieces of their past where they belong: behind them. In doing so, they are finally able to move forward with their lives. And maybe, just maybe, they'll discover a little something extra along the way. I hope you enjoy reading their story as much as I loved writing it.

Love,

Tina Beckett

ONE NIGHT WITH THE SICILIAN SURGEON

TINA BECKETT

MEDICAL ROMANCE

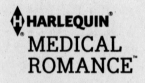

HARLEQUIN®
MEDICAL
ROMANCE™

Recycling programs for this product may not exist in your area.

ISBN-13: 978-1-335-40913-3

One Night with the Sicilian Surgeon

Copyright © 2022 by Tina Beckett

All rights reserved. No part of this book may be used or reproduced in any manner whatsoever without written permission except in the case of brief quotations embodied in critical articles and reviews.

This is a work of fiction. Names, characters, places and incidents are either the product of the author's imagination or are used fictitiously. Any resemblance to actual persons, living or dead, businesses, companies, events or locales is entirely coincidental.

This edition published by arrangement with Harlequin Books S.A.

For questions and comments about the quality of this book, please contact us at CustomerService@Harlequin.com.

Harlequin Enterprises ULC
22 Adelaide St. West, 41st Floor
Toronto, Ontario M5H 4E3, Canada
www.Harlequin.com

Printed in U.S.A.

Three-time Golden Heart® Award finalist **Tina Beckett** learned to pack her suitcases almost before she learned to read. Born to a military family, she has lived in the United States, Puerto Rico, Portugal and Brazil. In addition to traveling, Tina loves to cuddle with her pug, Alex, spend time with her family and hit the trails on her horse. Learn more about Tina from her website, or "friend" her on Facebook.

Books by Tina Beckett

Harlequin Medical Romance

The Island Clinic
How to Win the Surgeon's Heart

New York Bachelor's Club
Consequences of Their New York Night
The Trouble with the Tempting Doc

A Summer in São Paulo
One Hot Night with Dr. Cardoza

Miracle Baby for the Midwife
Risking It All for the Children's Doc
It Started with a Winter Kiss
Starting Over with the Single Dad
Their Reunion to Remember

Visit the Author Profile page
at Harlequin.com for more titles.

To my husband, who is always there for me.

PROLOGUE

Ugh! She was so tired of waiting. Especially with the questions rolling around in her head and the nausea that had pooled in her stomach.

Breandan Frost started as the door behind her creaked, a sense of trepidation sweeping through her. He was here. They could have things out before the wedding. If there was even to be a wedding.

Her long white dress hissed around her ankles as she turned quickly. Not Sergio.

She forced a smile as her dad's worried face came into focus. He wore his dark tuxedo in the same way he'd always worn his military uniforms, his bearing proud and unflappable.

"Dad, I can't talk about this anymore. Please. Not right now."

Her father had come into her dressing room about an hour earlier and, kissing her mom on the cheek, had asked if he could have a few moments alone with his daughter.

Instead of the pep talk she'd been expecting, he'd pulled out a tabloid with a headline that screamed an accusation.

Hotel Mogul Accused of Money Laundering!

All of a sudden, Sergio's secretiveness about his business dealings, an evasion that had made her more and more uneasy over the last month, seemed to click into place. Buried in the article was a picture of him at a New York restaurant with a beautiful blonde, his electric smile on full display. The second picture had been cropped to show the woman's bare foot curled around Bree's fiancé's ankle. The paper was still sitting on the vanity where she had sat and done her makeup.

When and if he arrived at the church, his explanation would determine whether she walked down that aisle as planned or walked out the door.

"I'm sorry, sweetheart. I'm not here to talk about what Sergio has or hasn't done."

Something else was wrong. Very wrong. "What is it? Is Mom okay?"

"She's fine, she just…" He dragged a hand across his silver hair. "Sergio was parked out front and—"

Her teeth clenched as another wave of sickness hit her system. She gave a half laugh. "I halfway thought he was standing me up. Maybe it would have been better if he had."

Growing up the child of an American military officer stationed in Italy had been confusing. At times, she'd felt kind of lost, like she didn't fit in on either side of the Atlantic. But she loved Italy, and eight years ago she'd made the difficult decision to stay and do her education in the place she'd come to love. Her first position as a perfusionist was set to begin soon after she came back from her honeymoon.

Honeymoon. The word sat like a rock in her brain.

Tabloids were all fake, weren't they? Except they'd known about her engagement before they'd even told their parents.

Her father didn't say anything.

Sometimes those gossip papers got it right. She forced out the words. "Where is he?"

"Come sit down, honey."

"No, I don't want to sit down. Just tell me." Her wedding dress suddenly felt tight, constricting her torso and forcing the air from her lungs. Dragging her veil away from her face, not caring if she damaged the delicate lace, her voice dropped to a whisper. "Tell me, Daddy. Please."

"I don't know where he is. Maybe he saw the papers. He drove away about twenty minutes ago and hasn't come back." The growled words made her wonder if her father had been hoping to waylay Sergio before he ever made it back to her.

The love she'd once felt for her fiancé— the love that had seemed to be faltering lately—went down for the third time.

He'd left her here to fend for himself.

She blinked, trying to process what her dad was saying. She'd always had problems committing to people or things, knowing that her dad could be transferred at a moment's notice, even though they'd been in

Italy for close to twenty years. But Sergio, the CFO of a top chain of hotels, had swept her off her feet. Their whirlwind romance had been featured in one of Naples's many newspapers, much to her chagrin.

"I tried calling his cell, but he didn't pick up."

The wedding was already running late—very late—and there were journalists outside with cameras and microphones who'd surely seen him arrive and then drive away. Her mom had tried to diffuse Bree's nervousness earlier, fussing over this and that until Bree had finally sent her out to her seat so that she could regain her composure. Her three bridesmaids were already in the foyer according to the text from her mom she'd received a few minutes ago.

"Does Mom know? About everything?"

"No. I didn't have the heart to tell her. She looked so happy this morning." A muscle in her dad's jaw worked as he tried to contain his emotions.

A blaze of anger scorched through her. Sergio wasn't just doing this to her. He was doing it to her family. To his!

Spinning around to the dressing table, she

snatched up her phone and found her fiancé's name, punching the call button. It rang four times, and then he picked up.

"Serge? Where are you? You need to come to—"

"I'm sorry, *Signorina*, this is Officer Cardulla. Who am I speaking with, please?"

That wasn't her fiancé's voice.

Although she'd lived in Italy most of her life, her brain suddenly couldn't decipher what the man was saying. Then the realization dawned—Sergio was with the police. She started shaking.

So he'd been arrested? The reports were true?

Switching to Italian, she answered. "Th-this is his fiancée, Bree Frost. Can I speak with Sergio, please?"

"I'm afraid that won't be possible."

"Wh-why not?"

"Because fifteen minutes ago your fiancé was killed in a single-vehicle accident. Please come, so we may speak in person."

Killed? Sergio was dead?

All her questions disappeared in the mist that swept across her eyes. Seeped into her soul. Sergio wasn't coming back to the church. Not now. Not ever.

A ludicrous thought came to her. Would the blonde in the picture grieve his death?

The phone fell from her hand, clattering on the tile surface of the floor and spinning away. She could hear the officer still calling out to her as tears filled her eyes and spilled over.

When her dad pulled her to him without a word, the floodgates opened, and she turned and wept into his brand-new tuxedo. Wept for the dreams that would never happen. Wept for Sergio's family and friends seated in the huge, ornate cathedral expecting to see his wide smile at any moment.

But most of all, she cried for the fact that she hadn't been able to see through his pretense.

But never again. She wasn't being taken in by a handsome face and convincing lies.

From now on, Bree was going to be on her guard, with her defenses on high alert. And before she pulled her heart off emotional bypass, she was going to block up whatever artery fed the so-called love center of her brain. From now on she was operating off pure reason.

Except right now, everything inside her was telling her to run as far and as fast as she could.

CHAPTER ONE

SICILY. BREE STEPPED off the plane in Catania less than six weeks after coming back from her honeymoon trip. The trip she'd made alone. Her father had had to whisk her out a back entrance of the church to avoid the photographers out front. In her desperation to get away and avoid having to talk to anyone, she'd decided to catch a plane to the island and hole up in what would have been their honeymoon suite.

But that first night had seen her in the hotel bar, downing one too many drinks. When a dark-haired man with intense eyes had pulled up the bar stool next to hers, she'd turned toward him, needing to drown out the pain of betrayal. One thing led to another, and she'd lost herself in the arms of a stranger on her honeymoon bed.

Strangely, that encounter had gotten her through the worst of the continued gossip columns, which also reported Sergio had had a lover on the side who'd come forward and said he'd planned to abandon his fiancée for his one true love. His family had declared everything to be a lie, suing multiple tabloids.

But it didn't matter. Naples and the life she'd planned with Sergio were now behind her. On a whim, she'd applied at a hospital in Catania and had been shocked when she'd gotten a call the day she returned from her honeymoon. They wanted her.

And she wanted them. Desperately.

So here she was.

Wisps of smoke had sifted from Mount Etna as her flight had neared the island. Whether the volcano was welcoming her or warning her away, she had no idea, but she'd probably find out soon enough.

The double doors at the front of the airport opened, and a wave of heat hit her, making her pause before she wheeled her bags outside. Okay, well, here she was. And not a moment too soon. Her first shift started just two days from now. But flights had been booked with tourists all clamoring to see the famous island. At least she'd made it and had even found a hotel that had an opening for a few weeks.

But this time, she'd be smarter about her stay on the island. No more one-night stands with strangers or being romanced by powerful men like Sergio. She was here to work. To avoid thinking about her past mistakes. She'd been so jittery, her stomach had been tied up in knots until she'd stepped on that plane. But at that moment, everything seemed to fall into place.

She was here now. And she was determined to make Sicily her home. No matter how hard it might prove to be.

Diego Pintor swept into the operating room for his first major procedure of the morning: replacing the aortic valve of thirty-year-old Sara Nirvana. With freshly scrubbed hands held away from his body, he waited as one of the surgical nurses helped him glove up. Then he moved over to the table, his eyes taking in his normal team, nodding to each of them before shifting his gaze to the panel where the new perfusionist was already in place, adjusting dials. She was from Naples, from what he'd been told. When she glanced up, he was surprised to see vivid green eyes peering at him…eyes that widened slightly as she took him in. Her cap and mask were already in place, so he couldn't tell anything else about her, but something jiggled in the back of his head before he forced his attention away from her.

The patient was already sedated, the drape over her chest revealing where the first incision would take place. "Let's get her prepped."

The room went into motion with people taking their positions, instruments gleaming under the bright lights in the space. He glanced again at the perfusionist, realizing he probably should have introduced himself and welcomed her to the team and to the hospital. But that could come afterward. Right now, he had a job to do.

He moved closer to the sedated patient and glanced down, saying a quick ritualistic prayer over the person before asking for his first instrument and making an incision. Then all thoughts were on the surgery at hand. Fifteen minutes later, he was through the sternum and the patient's beating heart was in view. It never failed to fill him with a sense of wonder at how deeply the body relied on this one organ to sustain all its functions, even the brain.

The perfusionist was watching him with expectant eyes. He nodded to acknowledge her. "Are you ready for bypass?"

"Whenever you give the word."

The sentence was spoken in precise Italian, and the quick Neapolitan accent confirmed her being from the Naples area, but there was something else just below the surface. Something tinglingly familiar. He could have sworn he'd heard that voice somewhere before, but that was impossible. He'd been born and raised in Catania, leaving only for some of the highly specialized portions of his surgical degree, so their paths couldn't have crossed. He shook off the weird sense of déjà vu as he prepared the patient to be transferred onto the bypass machine.

Five minutes later his patient's heart was still and unbeating in her chest, receiving oxygenated blood from a machine rather than pumping it through her body.

"I'll need the donor valve as soon as I get the pulmonary valve moved over." Diego was the only surgeon in Sicily who'd performed the complicated Ross procedure where the patient's own pulmonary valve was used to replace the aortic valve. A donor valve was then used to replace the pulmonary valve. The advantage was the donor valve wouldn't have to withstand the stress of the blood volume handled by the aorta.

He carefully freed the pulmonary valve from its position and sutured it into its new location. He glanced up at the perfusionist. "How are we doing?"

Those green eyes met his, and a flicker of panic went through them. "Doing?"

He realized she wasn't sure what he was asking. Hell, that's right. This was her first real position. He struggled to tamp down his impatience and clarified the question. "How long has she been on bypass?"

"Oh, of course." Her eyes went to the clock. "Forty-five minutes."

The longer a patient was on bypass, the more chance there was of something going wrong or the heart not restarting. He was still well within the limits. He nodded at her, frowning as he studied her again, before dismissing whatever it was that was bothering him about the newest member of his team.

She was replacing Miriam Steffani, who had just had a child and decided not to return to work for an indefinite amount of time. He'd long ago made a decision not to have children. Not to have permanent relationships. Medical school had taught him more than just medicine. As had his father.

And as the only surgeon on the island who performed this particular procedure, he was in high demand, and Diego wasn't willing to do what his dad had done and keep impossible hours while leaving his two young sons with his wife and expecting her to raise them.

Diego loved what he did, and after missing a girlfriend's birthday due to his hectic schedule, and discovering she'd found solace in someone else's arms, he knew he couldn't have it both ways. And to think otherwise would be selfish. That resolve had cost him his last relationship and probably any other relationship he might have in the future. Although he tried to make it clear that he wasn't interested in more than sharing a bed. Dammit. Not the time or place to think about this. Nor what had led him to have a one-night stand in a bar several weeks ago. A very hot one-night stand. His eyes shifted to the perfusionist before he yanked them back to the open chest in front of him.

"I'm ready for the donor valve."

Sometimes a valve taken from a pig or cow was used, but a human heart had come available at the last minute, so Diego had opted for that. It was the easiest transition and meant that blood thinners might not be needed.

The nurse in charge of the valve carefully transferred it out of the insulated container and handed it over. "Okay, here we go." This was the most delicate part, hoping that the replacement valve—which wasn't always an exact match size-wise—could be grafted into place with minimal adjustments.

He eyed the opening in the heart and the valve. The new valve was pretty damned close, maybe a hair too big. But that was better than it being much smaller than the patient's own valve had been.

Carefully setting the valve in place, he

made a slight adjustment and then called for the suture material. With fine, even stitches, he tested the tension of each one as he went, making sure there were no gaps that could cause a bleed later on. He also wanted a smooth joining that wouldn't encourage the formation of blood clots the way a puckered surface might. Twenty minutes later, the new valve was secured in place. He checked and double-checked both valve replacements before preparing to transfer control from bypass to the patient's own heart.

"Let's restore blood flow." He glanced up in time to see the perfusionist nod. Together they walked through the sequence of events, and within a minute the heart began beating on its own, even though it wasn't actually pumping blood yet. That would come in a minute. Diego gave another check to make sure the rhythm was even before saying, "Diverting flow to heart."

The first chamber of the heart filled and pumped with no leakage in any of the sutured vessels. They waited another minute or two and Diego said, "Let's wean her off the support."

The transfer of power was smooth, with

the perfusionist handing the work back over to the patient's repaired organ. He allowed a smile. "Good job, thank you."

Then it was all about removing the rib spreaders and wiring the sternum back together before suturing muscle and tissue in layers.

There. Done.

He glanced at the clock. Five hours. Not bad for replacing two valves. He took a step back and let the nurses start clearing away the surgical field.

"Excellent work, people." He let his gaze travel the room, noting the exhaustion on several of the faces. The perfusionist was busy at her table, flushing lines and discarding consumable items. She didn't look up this time. It was as if she'd dismissed him now that her part of the surgery was over. That was okay—he'd catch her when she left the room. He really had been rude not to formally introduce himself, and he couldn't keep referring to her as The Perfusionist. He should have at least looked up her name before stepping into the room. Yet another misstep on his part.

Once the patient stirred from the anesthesia and answered a simple question, he stripped off his PPE and exited the room. He would check on her again in recovery. But for now, he waited outside the door to the surgical suite, waiting as the patient was wheeled out, followed by each member of the team. Then there was no one. There was no way she could have made it past him without him seeing her, so with a frown he reentered the room. There she was. Still in her mask and surgical cap.

He went over to her, wondering if she was okay. Normally once the patient left, there was no need to keep on face masks. Except she'd removed her gloves. When she saw him, her eyes closed for a second before reopening…as if she'd been hoping he was already gone.

"I was rude," he said. "I didn't introduce myself or welcome you. I'm Diego Pintor. And you must be…"

There was a marked pause before she said in a low voice, "I'm Bree Frost."

There it was again, the strange undertones to her accent he'd noticed earlier, especially when she said her name. It wasn't a traditional Italian name, either. He put the pieces together.

He frowned, realizing what it was. "You're American?"

She nodded, and a weird churning started up in his gut. "My father works on the military base in Naples."

Naples. He'd been right about that. Then he backed up to the part about her father. And the fact that she was American.

Oh, hell, no. It couldn't be. The person from that night six weeks ago had been American. It had come through in a few of their more intimate moments. Suddenly he had to know. "Surgery's done. You can take off your hat. Your mask."

She blinked, then slowly reached up and tugged her mask down. Pink lips appeared. Lips he vividly remembered kissing. Lips that had kissed him…and more.

Then came the hat, and red hair came into view, although it was pulled back in a bun this afternoon. But there now was no mistaking who she was.

A tiny hint of anger spiraled up his chest. He'd had women throw themselves at him before, once they realized who he was. But he could have sworn there'd been no sense of recognition on her face that night in the bar. But there was only one way to find out. "Did you know who I was when I came into the bar?"

"What? No." Her teeth came down and bit her lip. "I had no idea. And I certainly wouldn't have…"

Her voice faded away, leaving him to fill in the blanks. He switched to English to prevent anyone who walked by from easily understanding the conversation. "You wouldn't have what? Slept with me?"

She stared at him for a moment. "Of course not. I had no idea we would be working together—or that we would even see each other again. I was in the middle of a crisis the week I was here on the island. I hadn't planned on coming back once I left, but then again—" her fingers clenched together, twisting as she continued "—I hadn't planned on applying for a job when I was here, either."

"So why did you?" He knew he sounded abrupt, but the thought of working with someone he'd slept with? Whom he thought he'd never see again? Well, it was damned inconvenient. Especially with the way the memories of their bodies straining together were flickering through his head like an old movie. And those memories were having a strange effect on him. One he didn't like.

"I—I needed a change of scenery."

Surely she hadn't come back hoping to somehow find him. "A change of scenery as in location? Or people?"

"Location." She closed her eyes for several seconds before reopening them. There was something about the color of them that made him want to stare at her. Her voice, though, pulled him back. "And people. Listen, I had no idea you worked at the hospital. In fact, I thought you might be a tourist, too, and that our paths would never cross again. To realize the doctor doing surgery was the same person who..." She glanced away.

"Which is why you didn't want to come out of the operating room. And why you kept your mask on. Surely you realized I would eventually see your face?"

She sighed. "I knew you would. I just hoped you wouldn't recognize me. And if you did, I wanted time to decide what to do."

"Do?"

"I think maybe I should resign. Go back to Naples. Or at least go somewhere else."

The thought that he might have made this hard for her—hard enough for her to give up a new job—didn't sit well with him. "Don't do that. We slept together. So what? As long as you don't want more than that, we're fine."

"Of course I don't want more than that." This time the anger was on her side. "Why do you think I wouldn't tell you my name that night?"

That was right. She hadn't. He'd introduced himself as Diego but hadn't included his last name. Then again, he'd been drinking. And so had she, so things were a bit muddled in his head. At least about what had transpired before they left the bar. What they had done afterward remained crystal clear. So clear that he had dreamed about her for a couple of weeks after their encounter.

"Let's reintroduce ourselves, then. As colleagues, this time." He held out his hand in the American form of greeting. "I'm Dr. Diego Pintor, chief of surgery here at the hospital."

She smiled and took his hand, the turning up of lips doing crazy things to his head. And when a dimple formed on the left side of her cheek, giving her an impish air, he had to release his grip to keep himself from reaching out to touch that mysterious crease.

"Nice to meet you. I'm Breandan Frost. Most people call me Bree, though, and I don't normally wear a mask when not working."

"Except in front of me."

"Evidently." Her smile widened. "And thanks for not getting any weird thoughts."

Weird thoughts. Did picturing the way she'd looked naked come under the category of weird? Yes. And inappropriate. But this situation was going to be salvageable. At least he hoped it would.

"No weird thoughts other than it's nice to finally know your name. Mystery solved."

Was it? There was still that life crisis she'd talked about, whatever that had been. But he wasn't going to ask. He'd been going through a type of crisis of his own. Or more like a reaffirmation of what he didn't want out of life—like a repeat of his own childhood. So he and his latest girlfriend—who had broached the subject of having a family and moving in together—had called it quits, and Diego had gone to the bar to seal that decision. And sleeping with someone else had seemed the perfect way to do that.

"Yes. Mystery solved." Some odd expression came over her face, and she blinked. "Would you excuse me, please?"

"Yes, of course."

Bree Frost whirled away from him and started down the hallway, her steps quick and light. A moment later, she disappeared around the corner, leaving him standing there puzzling over this whole strange encounter and wondering what had fueled her decision to leave Naples and come to Sicily. But that was something he had no intention of asking her.

CHAPTER TWO

BREE DRIED HER face with paper towels, glad that the splash of cold water had chased away the nausea and dread that had surged up as she'd been talking with Diego. She hadn't actually gotten sick, but for a second she'd thought she might, which was why she'd felt like she had to get away.

Leaning her hands on the sink, she stared at her reflection in the mirror. She was paler than normal, but other than that, there seemed to be nothing out of the ordinary.

Just this morning, though, her father had texted her letting her know that a formal investigation of Sergio's financials was underway. He wanted her to know before she read about it in the media. She'd immediately googled Serge's name and seen the report. Evidently the tabloids were telling the truth.

Except this time, rather than the blonde, this report had included a picture of them from the day of their engagement party. She was smiling up at him, wholly unaware of what was going to happen in a few months' time.

She vaguely wondered if this meant his family would drop their lawsuits against the other papers.

No wonder she didn't feel well. The news combined with the shock of seeing the man she'd slept with less than two days after her fiancé's death… What kind of person was she?

Never make life-changing decisions when you're grieving.

Wasn't that the advice they gave people? And now she'd made two—having a one-night stand and moving to an island where she knew no one.

Except only one of those decisions was a life changer, and that was moving to Sicily. Right now, though, she was glad she was far away from Naples. Glad she hadn't told anyone except her family where she was going, and she knew good and well they weren't going to reveal where she was. Hopefully the papers wouldn't renew their interest in her.

That shook her. Would they?

"Sergio, why?"

She swallowed. Was the car accident that claimed his life…? Had he…?

No. The Sergio she knew had loved life. It had to be a freak accident. He'd been trying to outrun whatever demons had been chasing him and had lost control of his car.

Well, nowadays newspapers were almost passé, even in Italy. Undoubtedly someone would eventually figure out who she was, but hopefully whatever the investigation was, it would blow over, since they couldn't prosecute a dead man.

And if didn't?

Another wave of nausea surfaced, making her drop her head and close her eyes until it passed. Fortunately, she didn't have any more scheduled surgeries today. She wasn't sure she wanted to face Diego or anyone else until she pulled herself together.

If she didn't know better, she'd say she was having an anxiety attack. She'd only had one other one and that had been the night of the wedding, when she'd found out her groom had not only lied, had not only fled the scene leaving her standing there in a state of shock, but he'd also cheated on her.

So what did she do?

For one thing, she was going to spend what was left of the day familiarizing herself with hospital policy and do some of the exploring she hadn't been able to do yesterday. And she was going to try not to think about the fact that six weeks ago, she'd spent her very last night with Sergio and soon afterward she'd had to face the reality that she was never going to see him again. Ever.

Once she got through this, she'd feel better. At least, that was her hope. If she didn't, then the next several weeks were going to be filled with trying to keep people from seeing the dark circles under her eyes and trying to feign that all was right with the world when it wasn't. And when she wasn't sure it ever would be again.

Diego booted up the computer on his desk and waited as it shifted through a screenshot of some kind of natural wonder of the world that was supposed to tempt you to click on it to learn more. Mount Etna was the only point in nature that he wanted to keep track of. One of the world's still-active volcanoes, it deposited quite a bit of ash on the island, sometimes more than others. And the plume of smoke coming from one several craters was thicker today that it had been yesterday.

His valve replacement patient from yesterday was doing fine—he'd checked on her in recovery about an hour ago, and she was stable, no signs of complications so far. And he had a two-hour lull before his next set of patients, unless he was called down for an emergency.

He clicked past the opening screen, typing in his password. Today's news flashed across the screen. His finger pulled the cursor to the top right of the screen to get off the internet when something caught his eyes. The CFO of one of the major hotel chains was under investigation for something. That's not what had grabbed his attention, though. Instead, it was the image just under the headlines.

Manache! A red-haired woman smiled up in adoration at a man, her hand splayed across his abdomen. On her ring finger was a huge rock. He froze. It was an engagement ring. His glance swept back to her face, hoping against hope that he was wrong, then he spied a telltale dimple. Even if she was just a lookalike, what were the chances that she'd have that exact dimple on her left cheek?

He'd slept with an engaged woman? There'd been no ring on her finger that night. The chill turned to anger.

His eyes raced back to the headline:

Dead CFO of Exclusive Marquis Hotel Chain Under Investigation.

The man was dead. Car accident. Diego slumped forward half in relief, scouring the story to see when the man had died. Did it make a difference? Hell, yes. It was the difference between Bree cheating on a troubled fiancé and her drowning her grief in booze and sex.

A day. He'd died a day before their encounter. A day after she was supposed to have married this man.

She'd said she was going through a life crisis. No kidding.

Had she found out about the investigation and called off the wedding? Unless he planned on asking her that question, he would probably never know. What he did know was that other people at the hospital were going to find out about this, so he hoped she was ready for sympathetic noises coming at her from all sides and maybe some hard questions. Maybe he should make sure.

Why? It was none of his business.

But her face and the way she'd tried to hide her identity from him had sent a wave of compassion through him. And that undulating emotion was back, urging him to warn her. She might not welcome it, but at least he would feel like he'd given her a heads-up.

He picked up his cell phone before realizing he didn't have her number. So he dialed the central number to the hospital and waited for someone to respond.

"This is Diego Pintor. Could you page Dr. Frost for me and ask her to give me a call?"

"Certainly."

"Thanks." He set his phone down on the desk and read the article from top to bottom. Sergio Morenz had managed the hotel with his dad for the past fifteen years. It looked like his father was denying that his son could be involved in skimming funds from the chain, but evidently the police thought the story had some credibility. And he'd stood Bree up at her wedding before running his car into a telephone pole. Suicide? The thought went through his head, even though the story didn't spell that out. But he pictured Bree in her wedding gown waiting on a groom who never showed up.

Accidenti. He could see why she'd needed to get away, saw why she'd wanted a change in venue. Was she involved in whatever her fiancé had been up to?

He didn't think so. The story was dated yesterday morning and made no mention of her other than a brief paragraph about their wedding.

His phone chirped, and a city code from outside Sicily appeared across his screen. That had to be her.

"Pintor here."

"Hi, this is Bree. You wanted me to call?"

"Yes." He paused, the words on the tip of his tongue before swallowing them down. This wasn't something that should be done over the phone. So he changed what he'd been about to say. "Would you have time to come up to my office?"

"Your office?"

The surprise he heard in her voice…

Dio Santo! Did she think he wanted her there for sex?

"I need to speak with you about something. I'd rather not do it over the phone."

There was a long pause, then she said. "Okay, can you tell me where you're located?"

"Third floor, number three twenty-two."

"I'll be there in about five minutes."

He said goodbye and then sat back in his chair, staring at his computer screen. Was he doing the right thing? His fingers scraped through his hair in a rough gesture, and he realized he hadn't gotten it cut in a while. Not that it mattered. He'd always worn it a little longer than was conventional. More out of lack of time than anything else.

It was almost ten minutes before she knocked on his door. "*Entrare.*" He switched to English. "Come in."

Bree barely opened the door, sliding in and pressing her back against it to shut it with a soft click. "You wanted to see me?"

She was pale, her face drawn, looking very different from the woman in the photograph. There was no dimple. No smile. In fact, she looked almost…ill.

"Are you okay?"

She made a sound that he took to mean yes.

Now that she was here, he had no idea how to broach the subject. A subject that was very much not his business.

"Sit." Realizing it sounded like a command, he softened the word. "Please."

Gliding over to one of the no-nonsense chairs in front of his desk, she did as he asked, although she didn't lean back and make herself comfortable. Instead, she looked like she could take flight at any moment. She didn't have on scrubs, like she'd worn in the operating room. Instead, she was wearing a floral blouse with some kind of fluttery little things that might have passed for sleeves, leaving her smooth shoulders on display, freckles scattered across her skin. The island summers were going to do a number on her.

Her hair wasn't confined in a bun today, but instead flowed down her back. This was the woman he recognized from the night at the bar. "No surgeries today?"

"Not so far. But perfusion is used for more than just surgical procedures."

"Of course." ECMO had been used during COVID to help rest lungs ravaged by the virus, and it could do the same for heart conditions like infective endocarditis and some lung diseases. The idea was to give tissue time to heal.

"Do we have another patient?" she asked.

"No. Before I say anything, I want you to know I'm not trying to pry, but this came up when I opened my browser." He refreshed his computer screen and turned the laptop to face her.

If he'd thought she was pale before, now her face drained of any remaining color.

"My dad called to warn me yesterday morning, and I looked it up."

So she already knew.

"I just want to say I'm sorry for your loss." Hell, he was doing the sympathetic noise thing that he'd been trying to prepare her for.

"Thank you." Her hands gripped together on the edge of his desk. "His death was sudden, and I had no idea about…that." She motioned toward the screen. "We were supposed to be married the day he died."

She didn't say anything about her fiancé standing her up.

He nodded, choosing his words carefully. "I wanted to let you know, in case other staff members see it. I thought you might want to prepare yourself for the possibility."

"I will. Thank you again. I didn't advertise that I was coming to Sicily, so hopefully reporters won't be able to find me and cause trouble for the hospital. I can't imagine why they would want to. I had no clue about Sergio's business dealings, although maybe I should have."

"Let me know if there's anything I can do. As head of surgery, I have a little bit of pull as far as the hospital goes."

"Thank you. I appreciate that. The last several weeks have been hard."

"I imagine. What made you want to come to Sicily?"

"After the wedding that never happened, I had the airline tickets in my purse, and the hotel reservations had already been made. I needed an escape, so I came. That was supposed to have been our honeymoon."

Before he could stop himself, he leaned forward in his chair and covered her hand with his. "Again, I'm so sorry. If I did anything that night that was inappropriate…"

"You didn't. Like I said, I needed to escape. You helped me do that. At least for part of a night." Her lips tipped up for a second before returning to neutral.

It was on the tip of his tongue to tell her that he'd needed to escape as well, but this was about her, not him. "How can I help now?"

She shook her head. "I don't think there's anything you—or anyone else—can do. I just have to hope the press loses interest quickly. Or at least in anything to do with me." A frown marred her brows. "If you think this will cause problems for the hospital, please tell me and—"

"It won't cause problems."

"And if someone finds out that I came here six weeks ago and remembers us leaving the bar or arriving at the hotel?"

He hadn't thought about that. But that wasn't her responsibility. She hadn't forced him to spend the night with her. They were both responsible for their actions. But it might make working together tricky. Fortunately, he didn't do the hiring and firing at the hospital, so it wouldn't look like some kind of pay-to-play situation where she slept with him to gain favor or vice versa.

"We tell the truth. That we're two consenting adults and that it's none of their damn business."

Her dimple reappeared. "I like the way you think."

He realized he was still touching her, and a current of electricity sizzled up his arm, arcing toward places that had the words *Consenting Adults* written all over them. He took his hand away under the pretext of turning his computer back around to face him. "I've always felt it better to play it straight with people."

He'd made it a point to do that, especially in his encounters with the opposite sex.

"I agree. And if Sergio had—" her shoulders twitched in what might have been a shrug "—well, wishing won't change anything at this point. So your thought is that we don't volunteer information, but if someone guesses, we don't bother denying it, either. Is that right?"

"That's what I'm saying. Are we in agreement?"

"Yes."

"Great." He leaned his elbows on his desk and looked at her. "If you start getting harassing phone calls, you'll let me know?"

"It's not your job to take care of my personal life."

"No, but it's my job to make sure you're not kept from doing what you need to for your job."

Bree sighed. "I really appreciate it. But I certainly hope it won't come to that."

"So do I. But you'll let me know."

"I will, I promise." She paused. "How is our patient?"

"She's doing great." With that, the conversation turned back toward the professional realm, and Diego was relieved. He'd done his duty, and that was that.

All he could hope was that they could leave what had happened in the past, where no member of the press—or anyone else— would dig it up again.

A week later, the nausea that had been like background noise for Bree was back with a vengeance.

She'd been under a lot of stress as the news of Sergio's exploits seemed to loom larger and more horrible by the day. Not only was the press digging into his professional life, but they'd discovered the juicy tidbits about his private life as well. And these weren't just the tabloids, but respected outlets. He hadn't had just one woman on the side, he'd had lots. Most of them call girls.

While he and Bree had been together.

And she'd had no idea. How could she have been so blind?

Even thinking those words made a flood of bile rush up her throat. She'd slept with him the night before the wedding. Thank heavens no one had expected her to go to his funeral, since too many people knew he'd been seen leaving he church parking lot on his way away from the wedding, not to it.

On the way to one of his escorts' houses?

Thinking like this would do her no good at all.

It was a horrible mess. She'd had her IUD removed two weeks before their wedding because Sergio had wanted to start a family right away, as soon as the wedding was in the books. She'd been so excited about the thought of a baby.

What if she'd gotten pregnant during that time? Thankfully, he'd used a condom so that people wouldn't try to count months... after all, his family was highly respected in Italy.

Ha! Maybe they were, but Sergio? Not so much. Not anymore. How could he be so very different from the man he'd portrayed himself as?

The queasiness got stronger. Ugh. Wandering into the bathroom, she opened the door to the vanity to get a washcloth and saw a box of unopened hygiene products. She'd bought them before arriving on the island.

She hadn't had a period since her IUD had been removed. That would have been...

She counted back to her doctor's appointment. Eight weeks ago. She swallowed. Her doctor had told her it could take up to six weeks for her periods to start up again. She'd passed that threshold by two weeks now.

Oh, God, she couldn't be pregnant. Not after everything that had happened. How many times had they had sex since it had been removed? Seven? Eight times?

Another thought came to mind, causing her to press the back of her hand against her mouth. She'd had sex with Diego during that time as well. More than once on that night. Three times. They'd used condoms, but what about the time spent swapping them out? She'd been so used to the extra protection afforded by her IUD that she hadn't given it any thought.

Until now.

With shaking hands, she grabbed the washcloth and wet it, drawing the cool cloth over her face and pressing it against her temples.

Surely not. Surely her body was still just adjusting. Six weeks was an estimate. She was just an outlier on that scale of norms. Right?

There was a history of blood clots in her family, so she'd opted not to go on the pill after having the device removed.

Because Sergio had wanted children right away.

And so had she.

But now? With the scandal surrounding him?

No. She did not want a kid growing up

with that stigma. And the thought of carrying his child, with everything she knew now? She sank onto lid of the toilet, burying her face in her hands.

"Okay, Bree, don't panic."

She needed to get a pregnancy test and take it, just to reassure herself that all was well.

And if it wasn't? Well, she would cross that bridge when she came to it. Or maybe she would just burn it to the ground and not cross it at all.

With that thought in mind, she exited her hotel and went to look for a taxi. Walking around in this heat didn't really appeal to her, especially not with how shaky she was suddenly feeling.

She also needed to start looking for an apartment if she was going to stay on the island. She couldn't stay in the hotel forever.

Motioning to a passing taxi, she took it to the nearest grocery store and went inside, plucking up a basket as she went. She might as well pick up a few things for dinner since her hotel room had a mini kitchen in it. Except her stomach just didn't feel like food right now.

Okay, maybe just the test. She found the aisle and perused the selections, her stomach getting tighter and tighter as she thought about the possibility that she might actually be pregnant. It would certainly explain the nausea. But so could a lot of other things.

All she could do right now was hope for the best. And plan for the worst.

Deciding to forgo the food, she grabbed a test and threw it into the basket and made her way to the front of the store. There were a couple of people in line in front of her, so, hooking her basket in the crook of her arm, she used her other hand to fish around in her purse for her wallet. Finding it, she removed it, glancing to see where in line she was. The person at the register was done, so the guy in front of her moved forward, putting the things from his basket on the conveyor belt, glancing back at her.

Oh, no!

No, no, no! The words screamed through her head.

Diego stood there, a smile coming to his face when he saw her. "Hi. Getting something for dinner tonight?"

Her tongue stuck to the roof of her mouth,

and no amount of trying would get it to budge. He glanced at her basket and stood there as his items slowly traveled away from him on the conveyor belt. For a minute no one moved.

Then his eyes slowly came up and met hers.

CHAPTER THREE

SOMEHOW, HE MANAGED to pay for his items and make his way out of the store. But *porca miseria*, there was no way he was going anywhere without some kind of explanation.

She'd had a pregnancy test in her basket.

His mind flew back over the weeks until he arrived at a number. Seven. Seven weeks since they'd slept together.

Words whipped through his head that he could not say out loud.

Maybe the test wasn't for her.

Who the hell else would it be for? She'd only moved to the island, what? A week ago?

She'd been engaged, so maybe she was worried she was carrying her fiancé's baby. Well, *merda*, Diego was worried that she might be carrying *his*!

The last thing he wanted was a child. He'd already thought that through and had come to a firm decision. No kids for him. Zero. Nonnegotiable. It was what had ended his first relationship—the one he'd had in medical school. And the mention of it had ended his last relationship. Well, he and Bree certainly did not have a relationship.

They'd used protection. That thought chanted in his head over and over again. He'd been responsible, just like he always was. But Selina had also used protection, so they'd been doubly protected.

Surely Bree had as well.

She finally came out of the store after what seemed like an eternity.

He wasted no time. "I think we need to talk."

There was no sign of her purchased item, but it was probably hidden away in her purse. Her eyes closed for a second before reopening. "Yes. I guess we do."

His insides did a quick twist that made him break out in a cold sweat.

"Not here. We can either go to a restaurant or go to my place or yours." The last thing he wanted was for what he said to be overheard.

"I don't want a public place, either. We can go to my hotel."

Had he really been hoping she would insist that this had nothing to do with him? Evidently, she wasn't so sure, because right now she looked like she was being led to the gallows.

Well, hell, that was where he felt like he was going. All that time of being so damned careful. Of being so sure he was never going to father children.

How would he even be sure it was his, if it turned out she was pregnant? He wouldn't, unless her fiancé had been sterile. Or she agreed to a paternity test.

Maybe she wasn't even planning to keep it.

Rather than bring relief, that thought made a part of his chest tighten. He should have had a vasectomy as soon as he'd made his decision, but with his work schedule, it was hard to find the time. If he had, though, none of this would have had any bearing on him.

He swung his two grocery bags into the

front seat of his car. "I'll follow you since I have no idea where you're staying, unless it's the same place you stayed the last time."

"No. It's not. I'm at the Grangier."

"Okay, I'll meet you there." He knew where the place was. It was purported to have an excellent view of Mount Etna, although he'd never stayed there, so he had no idea.

But he was glad she wasn't staying at the hotel where they'd spent the night together. He didn't want those memories clouding his judgment.

They made their way to a quiet area of town that was less touristy than some of the beach side resorts. There it was, the Grangier. An older building, there were three floors and all of them had balconies that looked fairly private. It looked more like an apartment complex than a hotel, actually. Finding a parking place in the shade and glad he hadn't bought anything at the store that would spoil in the heat, he got out of his car and met Bree in the parking lot.

"Did you buy it?"

She didn't ask what he was talking about, but instead gave a quick nod, her fingers tightening around the handle of her purse. "My room is up on the third floor."

They went up the elevator, and Bree reached in her purse, bringing out the key card and inserting it into the slot on the door. Something clicked and it swung open. Immediately Diego saw that this was more like a *monolocale* than a hotel room, since there was a kitchenette and living/bedroom all housed in the same space.

"Is this where you're planning to live while you're here?"

Her chin went up, and she stared at him for a second. "Is that a hint?"

"A hint?"

"That you would rather I leave?"

He frowned, having no idea what she meant. "Why would my question suggest that?"

She pulled in a deep breath and then let it out all at once. "I just thought if I ended up being pregnant, you might not want me working at the hospital."

"So you think you are."

She set her purse on a side table and motioned him to one of three pieces of furniture in the room, a futon and two upholstered chairs.

Choosing a chair, he sat and waited for her to do the same. When she sat on the futon, she sent him a shrug. "I don't know. Maybe. It's complicated."

Complicated was definitely one word for it. "If it turns out you are, any idea of whose it is?"

"Exactly how many partners do you think I've had?"

"I was not implying you've had many. But I can think of two."

For all he knew, it could have been months since she'd slept with her fiancé. Especially with some of the things he'd read about the man.

She bit her lip and leaned forward in her chair, bracing her forearms on her legs. "Let's not get ahead of ourselves. I might not even be. The doctor said it might be six weeks before I—"

He instantly recoiled, and she must have noticed, because her words stopped in their tracks.

"Were you on fertility drugs?" The thought that she might be trying to get pregnant—on purpose—hadn't even crossed his mind. Until just this second.

"No, but Sergio wanted children right away, as soon as we married, so I had my IUD taken out two weeks before the wedding. She said it might be six weeks before I got my period."

He did the math in his head. "And it's been eight." He didn't even want to ask this question. It was intrusive and low of him, but he needed to know. "Were you and Sergio…?"

"Intimate? Yes. And then there was you."

And then there was him. A man who'd stupidly noticed a woman in a bar who looked like she was in distress and had gone over to her. The rest was history. Or maybe not, depending on the outcome of that little test in her purse.

"We used protection."

"Yes. So did Sergio. Every time. He didn't want us getting pregnant until after the wedding so there'd be no hint of scandal." Her lips twisted. "It all seems kind of ludicrous now, after all that's happened."

He bet it did, since the dead man's name was linked to all sorts of other scandals. "What would you have done if you'd married that night, before all of this came out?"

Her eyes came up and met his. "I honestly don't know. Probably filed for an annulment. I had no idea he was involved in anything." Her hand went to her stomach in a protective move that she probably wasn't even aware of. "Does it sound awful if I say I hope it's not his?"

She was asking the wrong man. Because if it wasn't Sergio's, that only left one other possibility.

"I can understand why you wouldn't want it to be. What will you do?"

"I think I'm going to wait until I know for sure before I head down that road." She looked at him. "I'm really sorry, Diego."

"You didn't do anything wrong." But he had. There were consequences for everything in life. He'd found that out the hard way. Found out the hard way that he was just as capable of missing important occasions, just like all the band concerts, sporting events and family vacations that his father had opted to skip because of his work schedule.

And Angela had seen firsthand that the apple hadn't fallen far from the tree when he'd missed her birthday party their first semester of medical school. Only she hadn't put up with it, like his mom had. But she had paid the emotional price for his actions. And so had he.

What would his dad say if he knew he was the reason Diego didn't want children? Probably nothing. His death of a heart attack three years ago hadn't been a surprise, with the hours he put in at his job. But his mom had gotten smart after Diego and his brother were out of the house. She'd divorced him. And even then, it didn't change his father's behavior. He was just as distant toward his two boys as adults as he had been when they were younger.

"Do you mind if I take the test now, so we can get any awkwardness out of the way?"

He hadn't even considered being here. But then again, he hadn't considered this situation ever arising. Maybe it was time to make that appointment and put paid to this ever happening again. "You do what you feel you need to do."

In the end, it wasn't up to him to decide what she did if she was pregnant. What he did get to do was decide what part he would play if the test came back positive and if she decided not to terminate.

Those green eyes looked into his for a long moment, and it was all he could do not to look away. One thing he knew was he wasn't going to opt for his father's route and be an absentee parent. He was either all in. Or all out.

She finally broke the silence. "Do you want coffee? Something to drink?"

So she was going to do it. Take the test. Right here, right now. "I think I'm good. Thanks."

"I'll be back in a few minutes." Picking up her purse, she headed toward a door at the back of the room. It clicked shut, and he took a deep breath, blowing it out to release some of the tension that had been growing in his head. Except it was still there. Still revolving around a central question.

Did he have it in him to actually be a father? A real one?

He had no idea right now. So all he could do was wait and see what the results were.

Bree stood in the bathroom after taking the test, not sure why on earth she'd suggested he wait. She could feel his presence out there in the other room—had seen the trepidation in his eyes when he realized it might be his.

When she'd said she wanted to get this over with, she thought she could answer both their questions in one fell swoop, but since she wasn't sure what she wanted to do if the test were positive, or what she even *could* do here in Italy…

God. She'd wanted a baby just as badly as Sergio had seemed to. But could she carry through with it, knowing it might be his? How many partners had the man had over the course of their engagement?

But this baby would be half hers and wholly raised by her. Surely that would cancel out Sergio's influence other than just contributing DNA to the process.

The stick sat a foot or so away from where she stood. Ten minutes had passed. She was going to have to look at it at some point. And poor Diego was sitting out there waiting to hear the verdict. So, leaning over, she pulled the test toward her. One line would mean life would go on as it had for both her and Diego. Two lines would mean…

She looked at the readout. One bold blue line and…one slightly lighter line.

Pregnant. She was pregnant.

Gripping the test, she sank to the floor and stared at it, eyes blurring.

No crying, Bree.

There were noninvasive paternity tests nowadays that could be done during pregnancy that might at least put Diego's mind at ease. And she could know once and for all who the father was. But would it change her decision?

She didn't think so. But it would undoubtedly make a difference to Diego.

All she could do was go out there and face him, taking the test stick with her to prove she wasn't lying.

Why would he think she would? She didn't even know Diego. Not really. He'd been a wonderful lover the night they'd been together, but that didn't mean he wanted to father a child with her.

In fact, she'd never even asked him if he wanted kids. And the look on his face in the supermarket...

Holding the test down at her side, she quietly opened the door.

He hadn't heard her, that was evident in his posture, so she took a few seconds to study him. He was no longer in his chair. Instead he was over by the door to the balcony, looking out. He was unmoving, hands balled up by his sides, and his spine was rigid. It wasn't the view of Mount Etna he was thinking about. It was the result of the test.

She'd kept him waiting long enough.

"Diego."

He immediately turned around, his gaze on her face rather than what was in her hand. "It was positive."

It wasn't a question. It was a statement. "Yes. I am more than willing to do a paternity test."

He gave a visible swallow. "You're going to have the baby."

She realized she'd already come to a decision.

"I think so, yes." She walked over to him and touched his hand. "But this is a choice I'm making on my own. I would never presume that you agree or disagree. Or to play any role in the child's life, unless you want to."

He dragged a hand through his hair, causing the waves to turn riotous, making him look much younger than he probably was. Yet another thing she didn't know about him.

"How can I just sit back and do nothing?" he said.

Bree didn't think the question was directed at her, but rather at himself.

"You don't have to make any decisions right now. But think it through. Deliberately. Carefully. Did you plan to have children at some point?"

He hesitated, his glance going to her midsection before returning to her face. Then he slowly shook his head. "I'd decided not to."

He hadn't wanted children. At all?

"Then don't let this change that. There are a lot of single mothers out there."

"You are sure this is what you want. To have this baby, knowing what you know now about your fiancé?"

She paused before answering. "I think I do. I'm not getting any younger, and I have a lot of love to give. I have a stable position that I can continue to work at up until I'm ready to give birth. I'll need to get a house, of course, but there'd be plenty of time…"

She realized she was babbling, but it was something she tended to do when nervous.

If she had thought about it a little more, she realized she could have just kept quiet about being pregnant until later, and then when it was obvious, she could have pretended the baby was Sergio's and not put the decision on Diego at all. But would lying have been fair to him?

Besides, he'd seen that test in her basket and her brain hadn't been fully engaged when he'd told her they needed to talk. To have claimed Sergio as the father might have come across as totally unbelievable. He was a very intelligent man.

But he also didn't want kids.

Bree had always been a free spirit, not feeling the need to settle down with any man. She'd been fully fine with adopting or going to a sperm clinic when she did decide to have kids. But somehow Sergio had changed those plans. She realized she'd become almost a different person when she was with him. One she didn't necessarily like.

Little by little he'd made more and more of the decisions for her. And she'd let him. That wasn't like her at all.

When had that happened?

She wasn't sure. But what she did know was that it was time to take back control over her life and destiny and be true to herself. No matter what Diego chose to do. Or not do.

"Listen. No one knows we were together that night. We can just assume the baby is Sergio's and go about our lives. No one will know anything different."

"I would know."

Those words hit her in the pit of her stomach. They were low and rumbly and filled with just enough accusation in them to keep her knees from turning wobbly.

What did he mean by that?

"But if you don't want kids, wouldn't it be better to leave it ambiguous so that no one knows for sure who the father is? I don't know why you decided kids weren't for you, and I don't need to know. But I don't want you to feel pressured to take on a role you don't want. In fact, I'd rather you didn't, unless you're very sure you want to."

When he just looked at her, she bit her lip and continued. "Look, I know this is a lot to take in. And we don't even know that it's yours, is what I'm trying to say. We could leave it that way. Or we could meet again later and talk some more. No pressure."

He turned and glanced back out the window. "Yes, I think meeting again is a good idea. Maybe in a more neutral location. Have you been out to see Mount Etna yet?"

The change in subject threw her for a second. "No, but I thought I'd take a trip up there on one of my days off."

"Why don't we have our next meeting there?" He turned back to face her and then stepped closer, his hand touching the one that still held the pregnancy test. "And for what it's worth, I'm sorry for whatever part I played in this. Truly."

The warmth of his fingers took away some of the chill that had nothing to do with the air-conditioning in the room. "Don't be, Diego. I think what happened that night helped clear my head. Helped me see things with different eyes."

It was true. She'd been trapped in a fairy tale that wasn't rooted in reality. Coming to Sicily alone and sleeping with Diego had helped pop that bubble once and for all, setting her free.

His palm cupped her cheek. "I'm sorry that life dealt you such a sucky hand in Sergio."

The sincerity in his voice made a lump form in her throat.

"At least something good has come of it. I got a job in a place I'm coming to love." She leaned into his touch for a moment before pulling away, afraid she would get caught up in yet another fairy tale. This time one that couldn't come true. She didn't want to be with a man who didn't want kids. Because she did want them. And whether she parented those children on her own or with a partner was something that wouldn't be decided in these few moments. That partner wouldn't be him, so she did not need to get emotionally involved with someone who was out of reach and who wanted different things than she did. "I think going to Mount Etna is a good idea. How long do you want to take to think things through…to decide whether you want to know the baby's paternity or not? To me, it doesn't really matter."

Not entirely true, but true enough not to be a complete lie.

"How about next Tuesday?" He took an audible breath and then said. "But one thing is sure. I *do* want to know, Bree. And if I am the father, I want to bear some of the financial burden, even if you think it's best that I'm not actively involved in the baby's life."

"Absolutely not. I'm fine with you knowing who the father is. But if *you* choose not to take an active role in this child's life, then that's on you, not me. And if that's the case, I'd rather you not have any role at all, financial or otherwise."

CHAPTER FOUR

HE TEXTED HER two days later and asked if she'd be willing to go to Palermo to do the paternity testing. He'd done some research into the timing, and it appeared they could do it this early in the pregnancy. They didn't have to go together. And they probably wouldn't have the results back in time for their trip to Mount Etna, but at least they would be on their way to getting an answer. And he could think through what she'd said about it being on him if he didn't want to take an active role.

Did he really think it was okay to bear some of the financial burden while shouldering none of the emotional burden? Wasn't that exactly what his father had done?

He'd said it to be helpful, but her response had been right on target, and it had been the correct one. If he couldn't be all in, then he shouldn't dip his toe into the pool at all.

How had he felt, knowing his dad had left money for his education? He hadn't wanted it. Had in fact given the entire sum to charity and had worked his way through medical school entirely on his own.

So how could Diego have made that kind of an offer?

Guilt? He wasn't sure.

His phone pinged, and he glanced down at his desk where it lay. It was Bree.

Yes, I can do that. Do I need to make an appointment?

Even wanting the test done far away from his hometown was telling. But if the baby wasn't his, it would prevent rumors from making their way through the hospital. And with Selina living in the same town, it could turn ugly. After all, she'd mentioned children, and he'd shut her down. Had stopped spending time with her.

And if it turned out he was the father?

Then let the rumors fly. And he would tell Selina the truth—that it was an accident.

He picked up the phone.

We don't have to go together if it would be easier for you.

Yes. That might be easier. If you could make the arrangements, it might make it less complicated, since I'm sure I'll need your permission anyway for the results.

They settled on a day that would be better for her.

Don't forget to keep your schedule clear next Tuesday.

This time his phone rang. It was Bree. "Hi."

"I thought this might be easier than continuing to text. Are you sure you still want to go?"

"I am. I don't want to put things off too long." He didn't. The longer he drew this thing out, the harder it was going to be. Not just for him. But for her, too, as she made plans for the future.

"All right. Do you want to leave from the hospital?"

"How about if I pick you up and drop you home afterward? It would save you a trip and your hotel is on my way."

There was a pause. "I've been looking at houses, actually, so I'm not sure I'll be here on Tuesday."

That was fast. So she was going to move forward with or without his decision. But it made sense, since she'd want to have a more permanent space for the baby. "Any luck?"

"I saw a couple of nice ones yesterday. I'm kind of partial to the view here at the hotel, but I know that's not likely to happen wherever I live."

"Don't count it out just yet. My house has a view of the mountain."

"Interesting. I'll keep looking, then."

The thought crossed his mind to ask her if she wanted to move in with him, but he froze his jaw. That was crazy. He didn't know her. And he liked living alone. It was another of the reasons he and Selina had broken things off. She'd wanted to move in together, and the fact that that thought had never crossed his mind was telling.

Maybe because he'd moved in with his girlfriend from medical school and that had been a disaster. He'd barely had time for her. And then on her birthday, when he'd told her he didn't have time to celebrate with her, he'd changed his mind at the last minute and had come home to find her with someone else. That had shown him just how terrible he was at relationships.

And yet here he was about to make a life-changing decision about another kind of relationship—this one involving a child—in less than a week's time.

He couldn't offer to let her move in, but maybe he could steer her in the direction of available houses, if she was willing to let him help. "Do you want me to go with you to look at houses?"

"Why?"

The question was blunt but not unexpected. "Because I know this city and have a good idea what fair prices should look like."

There was a pause. "Let's talk about that on Tuesday, too."

Meaning she didn't want to talk about it now. "Sounds good. Are you scrubbing in on my surgery today?"

He had a heart bypass patient scheduled who might or might not need to go on a heart/lung machine. It depended on how close to the heart he would need to get in rerouting the blood supply.

"I am, so I'll see you this afternoon?"

"Yep. I'll see you then." With that, they said their goodbyes.

Diego leaned back in his chair and looked at the phone. If he decided not to parent, he needed to stick to that decision and not waver. Because it wasn't fair to Bree or the baby to have him duck in and out of their lives. And he was pretty sure she would cut him off the first time he tried to do that.

So if ever he needed to detach his emotions and make a rational, thoughtful decision, it was now. And that's what he planned to do.

The surgery yesterday had gone well. So well that they hadn't needed to put the patient on the bypass machine, so she'd been able to watch Diego work. His hands were sure and confident. No second-guessing with this man. So she could bet when he made a decision, he didn't back down from it.

That actually helped her to feel better. Because whereas she could be all over the place as far as thinking and rethinking and triple thinking, Diego evidently didn't. So she wouldn't have to worry about him changing his mind midstream.

After the surgery he'd told her that he'd been able to get them both appointments for paternity testing today. They could drive separately, since he knew that was her preference. But in keeping with her personality, she told him it was okay, that they could ride together if he thought that would help the process.

So here she was standing in front of the hospital waiting for him to pick her up. It didn't take long to see someone creeping up to the curb in a sleek sports car. Sergio had been all about those. In fact, speed had been a factor in the single-car accident that claimed his life. She tensed. Would Diego feel the need to go fast as well?

She slid into the passenger seat, the leather cradling her in a way that somehow reassured her. Buckling herself in, she glanced at him. "How far is Palermo from here?"

"About a two-hour drive. I thought we might stop on the way back and get something to eat."

"Thanks, that would be great." She hadn't felt much like eating today, but having him drive actually took some of the pressure off her to get there and find the place.

"Looks like it's blood draws for both of us, since it's still early in the pregnancy."

She turned to look at him. "Are you sure you want to do this?"

A hint of a frown appeared. "Do what? Find out who the father is? Absolutely."

It would undoubtedly save him some angst in decision making if it turned out the baby wasn't his. And if the baby was?

Then Diego had a decision to make. She'd already made hers. And this was one decision she wasn't waffling on.

The bangles on her wrist jingled as she clasped her hands together.

"You were smart in bringing a change of clothes to work."

"You look fine," she said. "I had on scrubs and clogs. At least you look like an ordinary citizen."

He did. He had on a white button-down

shirt that was loose and flowing and reminded her of an artist's attire. All he lacked were the cream linen slacks and bare feet.

She'd like him barefooted.

A shiver ran over her as her mind conjured up an image of Diego with his curly hair mussed from sleep, sitting on a bar stool with the clothes she'd just thought of. Only the shirt would be undone, revealing a hint of the dragon she'd seen tattooed on his upper right arm the night they'd been together. His feet—tanned and naked—might be propped on the stool's footrest. He would reach for her hips and pull her toward him, his eyes searching hers. And as their bodies connected, she would feel every inch of his…

She shook herself back to the present with a sense of horror, her face burning as she realized he'd asked her something.

"I'm sorry, I missed that."

"I asked if you'd had any luck finding a house?"

"Oh, I think so. I was going to run it by you, since you said you know about pricing and the areas in the city. Maybe when we're waiting on them to call us in for our tests."

And she needed to check on whether or not the house had bar stools.

A laugh came out before she could stop it.

"Something funny about that?"

"No, sorry." She needed to stop this before he figured out what she was thinking about. Maybe she would do better to worry about what the results of the test would be. She hadn't wanted it to be Sergio's, but maybe it was better that it was. She could honestly tell her son or daughter that their father had died in a car accident, rather than figure out how to explain that Diego simply hadn't wanted to be a father.

He glanced at her. "Where is it?"

"It?"

"The house."

Of course. What else would he be talking about? "About three blocks west of where I'm staying now."

"That's not too far from where I live. We can drive by it when we're done in Palermo, if you'd like."

Maybe coming together wasn't such a good idea. Her nerves were acting up. But at least her stomach had been stable so far this afternoon. "I don't want to inconvenience you."

"It won't be. Is the view what you were hoping for?"

"Yes, it has a nice big balcony off the upstairs bedroom. There's even a ceiling fan out there and plenty of shade."

He glanced over. "It sounds ideal. There's another bedroom for the...baby, I take it."

There'd been an awkward pause before he said the word. If he couldn't even bring himself to utter *baby*, how would he be when there was an actual human being to go along with that word?

She fiddled with her bracelets, the clinking sound helping to calm her.

"Yep, it has three bedrooms. It'll be nice to have a little more space than the hotel, which is more like a studio—what is the word in Italian?"

"*Monolocale* is I think what you call a studio. You have a great view at the hotel, though."

"It is pretty spectacular. The house I'm looking at has a view of Etna, but it isn't as clear a line of sight as the hotel. Probably because the house is only two stories high and is attached to neighboring homes on both sides."

"A lot of the homes here are. Mine is as well."

The road went up as they neared one of the mountains, and the green that surrounded them was spectacular. "It's gorgeous here. Mainland Italy is as well, but this is different."

"It's hard for me to see it through the eyes of someone who hasn't lived here their entire life. If you haven't been to the beach in Catania, it's worth the trip."

"But is it worth the sand?" She grinned at him, nose crinkling with feigned disgust.

"You don't like sand?"

"Let's just say if I had the choice between a beach or a mountain, the mountain would win hands down."

"Oh, but the beach has its charms. Especially at night. In the dark." He smiled back at her, and the sight made her shiver. The man was so intense that even his smile carried that aura. And he was far too sexy.

The image in her brain shifted from Diego on a bar stool to Diego ankle-deep in the ocean, beckoning her toward him. Suddenly the idea of sand didn't seem so heinous.

She swallowed. "Does it?"

"It does. But good thing we have that trip planned to Etna on Tuesday. No sand."

She suddenly wanted to see the beach he was talking about. At night. With that sand she claimed to dislike clinging to the bare skin of Diego's back.

What was with her picturing him without clothes?

God, she was having a baby. About to find out who the father was. How could she think about anything other than that? She couldn't control much about the situation, but she could damn well concentrate on what she could control. Like where she was going to live and what she was going to do about childcare once the baby was in her arms.

A wave of love swept over her. She was actually going to get to hold this child. Cradle it deep in the night. In the end, did it really matter who the father was? This was *her* baby. *Her* responsibility. A fierce sense of protectiveness burrowed into her chest. She was going to do the absolute best she could to make sure this child never doubted her love. Never doubted that she would give her or him her all.

Out of the corner of her eye, she noted that Diego had looked her way several times. She realized he was waiting for her to respond to his earlier comment about the beach. "Yes, good thing we're going to Etna instead."

If their reasons for going up the mountain weren't so serious, she would be excited about the trip. As it was, it felt like he was going to render judgment on whether or not he was willing to be his baby's father. Of course, he'd never actually said he wouldn't. In fact, she was the one who had given him an ultimatum of sorts. But she needed to know. For sure. She didn't want Diego to start out strong and then disappear from his child's life two or three years down the line. Wasn't that part of focusing on what she could control? Suddenly she needed to know.

"How much farther is it to Palermo?"

He glanced at her in concern, his smile fading. "Are you feeling okay?"

"Yes, I'm fine." She decided to be honest

without sharing her reasons. "I'm curious, that's all."

"About twenty-five minutes. So not much farther."

They arrived in the city, and it was a lot bigger than Catania, both in size and in feel. And the roads were crazy busy. Worse than in Catania. She was glad she hadn't attempted this alone. She would get used to the crush, and Naples had traffic problems of its own, just like every big city. "Do you know where the hospital is?"

"I do. I did part of my rotation here. It was an option when I was in medical school, and I wanted to see how things worked in hospitals outside Catania."

"And yet you decided to stay in Catania?"

"I can't imagine living anywhere else, honestly."

That statement gave her pause. And if he were the father and she decided she wanted to move back to the mainland? He would stay in Catania. Why wouldn't he? Just because he might be the baby's father, that didn't mean they were involved with each other. He didn't need to live near her to be a part of the child's life. Right?

So why did that thought leave her so deflated?

Ten minutes later they were pulling into the parking lot of a large, modern-looking hospital. "Nice."

"It's one of the best hospitals in Sicily." He parked the car, and they got out, walking toward the entrance.

Nerves were sending a herd of elephants into her belly that seemed to stomp with every beat of her heart—which was getting quicker by the second. She only realized she'd slowed her pace when Diego had to stop for a second to let her catch up.

"Okay?"

"Just nervous, that's all."

One side of his mouth went up. "Me, too, if that helps."

Not really, because the reason for his nerves was probably different than hers. She was nervous about him being or not being a father. And he was probably nervous that he *would* be a father.

More and more she was wondering if she'd done the right thing. Not just about coming here together, but about telling him she was pregnant. Kind of hard to hide when you're caught with the test in your basket.

But she could have quit and moved away, never letting him know where she was. That felt dishonest, though. And if the baby grew up and went looking for him?

She shivered at what his reaction might be.

Some of that fear must have made itself known, because he reached for her hand, squeezing it and then letting it go. "It shouldn't take long. Did you eat lunch?"

She thought back and came up blank. "No, I just grabbed a snack from the snack bar."

"Then I'm doubly glad we're stopping on the way back."

They arrived at the lab, and she went up to the desk with Diego, somehow feeling embarrassed. Most women knew who the father of their child was. But the receptionist was kind and professional, not looking at her any differently than she might anyone else. That helped settle her nerves.

"We'll call you back in just a minute."

She was really hoping they called them back separately.

Almost before they found seats in the crowded waiting room, Bree heard her name. She avoided looking at Diego as she headed toward the open door where a woman dressed in scrubs waited.

"Right back this way."

She did her best to smile at the woman. "With the number of patients out there, I'm surprised it was this quick."

"Most of them are here for other types of testing. And we're quick back here in phlebotomy."

"Thanks."

The nurse's kind nature and wide smile helped put her at ease. "How long have you been in Sicily?"

"That obvious, huh?"

"Your accent." She motioned Bree to a seat, putting the arm up so she could rest her right forearm on it. "And your name, actually."

"I was born in the US but have lived in Naples for much of my life. I decided to get my education here and have actually just started working at Ospedale Maria di Concepción."

Her brows went up. "My best friend works there."

Bree immediately tensed, but the woman put her hand on her arm. "Don't worry. I won't say anything. I wouldn't even if there weren't laws in place. I know how it feels to go through this."

"You do?"

"Yes. I'm Teresina, by the way." She smiled. "And my test came out the way I needed it to. I hope yours does as well."

"Thanks." Bree wasn't sure how she wanted her test to come out. But she was hopeful that whoever the father was, it would end up the way it should.

After that, Teresina was all business, cuffing her upper arm with elastic tubing and sliding the needle home with the ease of someone who had done this thousands of times. She probably had. She drew one vial of blood then pulled the syringe free, putting a Band-Aid over the site. "There you go. You should get the results back in a week. You filled out your contact information?"

"Um, I didn't, but…" She licked her lips.

"Could you read me what you have down for me?"

"Certainly." The phlebotomist went over to her computer and pulled up the file, reading off the address. Diego had a good memory. He'd only been to her place once. Or maybe he'd looked it up through Human Resources. No, she didn't think he would have done that, because it probably would have shown the search and his access would have been noted. At least at the hospital she'd trained at it would have been.

"That's correct. Thanks for checking."

"Not a problem." Teresina paused, then said; "It is absolutely none of my business. But if something violent happened…if you need help…"

It took her a second to puzzle through what the woman was saying. Then her heart ached, remembering what she'd said about her own test coming back the way she'd needed it to. "I'm fine. My pregnancy is the result of a failed condom. Nothing more than that."

"Okay, good. My stomach knots up every time someone comes in for one of these.

Because in my case..." The woman's eyes watered.

Bree nodded. "I'm truly glad your results were what you wanted."

"Me, too. My husband's a good man and told me I didn't need to have it done, that it didn't matter to him. That maybe it would be better if I didn't know. But it mattered to me." She blew out a breath. "Anyway, I have no idea why I just shared all of that. If you're ever back in Palermo, please look me up."

"Thank you. I'll do that. Do you have a card?"

Teresina produced one from the pocket of her scrubs and handed it to her. "I'm serious."

"I really appreciate it, and I think I'll take you up on it." Despite the circumstances, Bree felt like she'd just met her first friend in Sicily. And God knew she needed one. One who was totally separate from her hospital.

When she returned to the waiting room, Diego was gone. For a second, her stomach clenched, and she wondered if he'd taken off and left her, just like Sergio had. No. That was ridiculous. Teresina had said that her department was in a lull, so he'd surely been called back.

Sure enough, three minutes later he was back, and despite all her rationalizations, she breathed a sigh of relief.

"All done?" he asked.

"I am. Teresina said it would take about a week to get the results."

"Teresina?"

She could have kicked herself for saying the woman's name. "She drew my blood."

Who knew? She might decide to have her baby at this hospital, well away from any prying eyes. Especially if Diego decided to bow out.

"Ah, okay. I was told a week as well."

"So now we wait." Somehow saying the words gave them a finality that lodged in her chest and stuck there long after they'd left the hospital.

A week. A week to figure out how to be a dad.

Hell, if he hadn't been able to figure it out in all those years since his medical school romance, why did he think he could figure it out in seven short days?

Well, technically it wasn't seven days. If the baby was his, he'd have until the child was born before making plans. But it wasn't fair to Bree to make her wait that long. She needed to prepare for this baby. With or without him.

Diego had never been one to shirk responsibility. If anything, it was the opposite. But this time it wasn't just about him. It was about Bree and the baby as well.

If Angela, his girlfriend from med school, had gotten pregnant, it might have been a more straightforward path. He could have just married her and muddled through the best he could. But after seeing what his absence had done to her, what she'd needed to do to get what she needed, he'd realized even as a partner, he hadn't been the best choice.

And it was why he'd ended things with Selina as soon as she started wanting more. Because he just didn't think he had more in him. He was in surgery or planning a surgery on most days and Selina, just like Angela, would be stuck with what was left of him at the end of a long day. Which wasn't much.

He could have cut back on his schedule

and sent some of his caseload to other area hospitals, but he'd chosen not to. Maybe because he'd wanted Selina to see the reality up front.

So, if he wasn't marriage material, how did he expect to be father material?

Except in a relationship there was an out. You could never undo the ties of fatherhood.

Maybe the best idea was to go through this next week with the assumption that the baby was his. He could mull through things as if this were the real thing. Figure out how he could play it differently than his father, or if that was even a possibility for him.

Then if it turned out the baby was Sergio's, he'd be off the hook. Ha! And if that didn't sound like the thought of a selfish bastard.

But wasn't he?

And if he was selfish in his thoughts, what would make him different in the life of an actual living human being? Was selfishness programmed into one's DNA? He had no idea, but God, he hoped not.

To take his mind off his musings, he glanced over. "There's a town not far from here called Campofelice di Roccella. I know you're not much of a beach person, but it's a cute little beachside town that has a great restaurant with a view."

She smiled over at him, that dimple giving a flirtatious wink that she was totally unaware of. "Does 'beachside' mean we would have to eat on the beach and pick sand out of our teeth?"

"Nothing like that. Trust me?"

Her head tilted, and she looked at him for a minute. "Yes. I do."

The words sent a shiver through him. Such trust, so easily given. It had gotten her hurt not too many weeks ago by a man she should have been able to trust. She didn't deserve to be hurt like that again. So he needed to tread lightly. Starting with those words.

"I promise no picking sand out of your teeth, how's that?"

"That will work."

They arrived in the town and Diego drove partway up a mountain to get to Pasta in Mare, a place where they made homemade pasta and had a spectacular view of water and mountains alike. He found a parking place, and they got out of the car. Bree went over to the rough wood railing and looked out, leaning her forearms on the banister.

"This is really lovely, Diego. A mountain with a view of the beach. What more could anyone ask for?"

He came to stand beside her, a strange, sharp longing coming over him. He pushed it to the side. Just because you wanted something didn't mean you should have it. Hadn't he proved that by sleeping with Bree? He'd wanted her and had thought it was something flip, something he could forget about the next day. The problem was, he hadn't forgotten. And to see her again...

Well, he needed to be careful. His dad had evidently wanted marriage. Had wanted a family. So what had happened? Had the reality of the day-to-day grind worn him down? Or had he simply done what was expected of him by society and had kids? Things in the world had changed since then, but there were still societal pressures.

So as he stood there looking at the beautiful view, next to an even more beautiful woman, he needed to make sure he separated wants from shoulds and was very careful that he kept them as far apart as he could.

CHAPTER FIVE

IT DIDN'T TAKE long to be seated, since they'd arrived at the restaurant in between the lunch and dinner rushes, when the wait times could be phenomenal. Not only to be seated but also to be served, since this place was famous for its pasta and the view, which Bree had had a hard time pulling herself away from.

He was glad she liked it.

The waiter came over and presented them with wine menus. Diego glanced up in time to see pink infusing Bree's face. He knew exactly why. She wasn't supposed to drink because of the pregnancy. And although wine could be ordered by the glass, it was more customary to order a bottle.

Diego took the lead. "I'll just have a water, please."

"Yes, I'll have the same." The relief in her voice was palpable. A sense of warmth went through him. One right choice down. A million more to go.

Or maybe it wasn't because of pregnancy. Maybe she was worried that he might drink too much. Look at how he'd been the night they'd slept together. They'd both drunk more than was safe for driving.

He looked at her. "Just to be clear, I would never do anything to put my passenger or other vehicles in peril."

"Oh, I didn't mean… It's just I can't…"

This time it was Diego who felt relief. "I understand. I just wanted to make sure you knew."

"Thank you."

Car accidents were probably a difficult subject for her anyway, because of her fiancé's death.

The waiter had left food menus as well, and he passed her one.

She glanced at it. "What do you recommend?"

"The swordfish is very good, as is *sarde alla griglia*. Italian sardines are nothing like the canned ones from America, however."

"I grew up in Italy, remember? I love the sardines here."

"Good. The squid is also very nice."

She laughed. "Okay, I grew up in Italy but still haven't gotten past anything with tentacles."

He liked when she laughed. The bangles on her wrist jingled with the movement like the wind chimes from his mother's porch. Soft. Comforting.

And the way her mouth curved, showing off white teeth and that treacherous dimple. It was no wonder he hadn't been able to resist her at the bar that night.

"I bet you would like these." As much as he liked her smile? He doubted that was possible.

"I don't know…"

He grinned, leaning forward. "I could order some for myself and you could take the tiniest of bites."

Dios, those words had come out in a husky voice that he didn't recognize. And they made all sorts of images slide through his head.

"Hmm…maybe. How about if I order the sardines, and you order your tentacles, and we share." Her dimple winked again. "Unless I don't like yours, then all bets are off."

"Somehow I think you will like mine very much."

Her face bloomed with color, making him realize he wasn't the only one who was feeling these odd vibes—ones he was having trouble controlling. Thankfully the waiter came with their glasses and a large pitcher filled with water, sliced lemons and plenty of ice. It was hot outside, and the windows to the restaurant were open. But with the sea air flooding the space and the large ceiling fans above them, it was warm but not uncomfortably so. And he loved the smell of the water.

The waiter asked if they were ready to order. He raised his brows at Bree. "What do you think? Are you willing to share?"

"Let's go for it."

His eyes met hers. "Yes. Let's."

Diego placed their order, asking for stuffed mushrooms as an appetizer. Once the waiter left, he poured water in their glasses. "Seriously, if you don't like the squid, don't feel like you have to eat them."

"Don't worry. I won't." Her bangles

sounded again as she reached for her glass, making something inside him tighten. "I'll try them. Just no promises."

"I'd never ask you to promise."

They talked about work for the next fifteen minutes until their appetizers arrived. Bree cut into one of the mushrooms and popped it into her mouth. Her eyes widened, and he looked at her in alarm.

"You don't like it?"

She finished chewing and swallowed. "It's amazing. I love it! Seriously."

"You know raw seafood is not recommended during pregnancy." The words that came out of his mouth were ones he didn't even recognize, and he had no idea why he'd said them.

"I didn't order my food raw." She drew the words out in a way that said she was puzzled. As well she should be.

"Sorry. I have no idea why I said that, other than being a doctor."

"It's okay. I already figured that, like alcohol, sushi was off the menu. But thanks for your concern."

The words were said in a light tone, but there was a hint of warning behind them.

And she was right. Unless he could convince her to let him be a part of this child's life—and hers—he had no right to dictate anything to her. Actually, even if he did take an active role, it wasn't his job to police her food or anything else. Which wasn't what he was trying to do, but he could see how she might take it that way.

There was a subtle shift in atmosphere that made conversation difficult for a few minutes before she asked about the decor on the walls. Once they made it back onto neutral ground, things seemed to be okay. At least for now.

They finished the plate of appetizers just as their main dish arrived at the table. The sardines were nicely grilled to a golden color, and in the Italian way, their heads were still on. "Wow, these look fantastic."

"They taste as good as they look, if I remember right."

She glanced at his plate. "Okay, that doesn't look as scary as I expected. If I could just have a part of it that isn't curled and doesn't have suckers…" She bit her lip as if knowing it was a strange request. But it was an endearing gesture that made him smile, glad things between them seemed to be back on decent footing. He didn't know why that was so important to him, but it was.

"Not curled and no suckers, coming right up." These particular squid did not have long tentacles, and so it was easy to cut several chunks from the upper portion of the seafood, passing them over to her and allowing her to put one of the large sardines onto his plate. His mouth watered.

Campofelice di Roccella was one of his favorite towns, although his last girlfriend had never been a big fan of the place. Somehow he liked that Bree could find the beauty in the town.

She expertly slid her knife between the flesh and bones of one of her sardines and laid it on her plate, cutting off a portion.

"It's so strange," he said, "to see you do that with no hesitation."

"Why?"

"I'm not exactly sure."

She smiled, somehow seeming to guess that it was because she was American. "I've lived in Italy a lot longer than I ever lived in the States." She finished a bite of her fish before continuing. "But it's weird to feel like I somehow have a foot in two places but don't truly belong in either of them."

She'd used a typical Italian expression when she said it. "I think you're more Italian than you give yourself credit for. If not for your name and the tiniest difference in inflection when you talk, I never would have guessed you weren't from Naples."

"I think people outside Italy have this caricature in their heads of what people here look like. It's not like I'm the lone redhead in the country."

She was right. Just like in any nation, Italians came in all shapes, sizes and colors. It's what made the human race beautiful. "You're right. Just like the stereotypes people attribute to Sicily."

"Those stereotypes are nothing close to reality. It's beautiful here. Even more than I imagined."

"The beauty here is more than I imagined, too." He was talking about Sicily, but he was including the woman seated across from him in that statement. She was gorgeous. With the light of the sun behind her, it gave her hair an almost golden appearance.

Her eyes met his for a few seconds before traveling back to her plate. "Moment of truth." She speared a piece of the squid on her plate and took a deep breath before sliding it into her mouth. She chewed a second or two, her brows going up as her throat moved to swallow. "Well, okay, I didn't expect that."

"What? Do you actually *like* something you'd once claimed you never would try?"

He said the question and immediately tensed. Wasn't that what he'd done with the idea of having kids? Said he never would? Eating squid and taking on a lifetime commitment and doing it justice were two different things, though.

Her grin was spontaneous and contagious, making him forget his moment of reflection. "It's definitely not as tough as I expected it to be. Almost like a scallop."

"Yes. The trick with calamari is to either cook it quickly, before it has a chance to get tough, or to cook it for a long time until it becomes tender."

Maybe Diego was in the second category. Maybe he needed to be flung into the fire for a long time before he could become tender. Before he learned how to be nurturing. Except that took time. And he just wasn't sure he had enough of it.

"I'm not sure I could ever get used to the tentacles, but the squid itself is quite good." As if to prove her point, she ate another piece, followed by an olive from a little bowl on the side of the table. "I'm going to be very full, though."

He thought of something. "How's your queasiness?"

"It's been okay, except in the mornings or when I'm placed in a stressful situation."

So she didn't find being here in the restaurant with him stressful. He liked that.

They ate for a few more minutes, and the mood between them had lightened considerably since they'd left the hospital. He could understand why. They'd taken the tests and there was nothing they could do to change the outcome, so worrying accomplished nothing.

Do you actually like something you once said "never" to? If only it were as easy as he'd made it sound.

The waiter appeared at their table with another, smaller, menu. *"Vuoi un dolce?"*

Diego looked at her in question. "What do you think? Dessert?"

"I don't think I can eat another bite, but you go ahead."

He shook his head at the waiter. "I think just the bill, please."

Bree looked conflicted, as if she was going to contradict him, but she didn't say anything until after the waiter left. "I'd planned on buying my own meal. So we can just split the check."

"Please let me. I enjoyed showing you one of my favorite spots in Sicily."

She hesitated before nodding. "Okay. This time. But next time is on me."

Was there going to be a next time? Something about the thought of that made a warm wash of pleasure run through him. Of course, they were going to Mount Etna on Tuesday, so it was likely they would eat together then as well.

He paid the bill, and then they were out of the restaurant. The sun was beginning to sink on the horizon, turning the sky to an assortment of reds and pinks, painting the tips of the mountains in the same colors.

"Look at that," Bree murmured, standing

at the railing. "It's so beautiful. Can we stay here for just a minute?"

Yes, they could. They could stay for as long as she liked. Anything to keep from returning to the reality of his life, which had now taken a turn that was…unexpected. Although, that word sounded too tame for the wild ride he was about to embark on.

And what about her? What was she thinking?

He half turned toward her, propping his hip against the low wall. "Are you doing okay, Bree? I didn't think to ask."

She stared out at the horizon. "I'm not sure. I've always wanted children, but this wasn't quite how I envisioned having them. When Sergio died and I realized who he was, exactly…well, who knows how long I would have waited if left to my own devices? Maybe it would have been too late by the time I was finally ready to try. I'm hoping this will work out the way it should have." She turned to face him. "And I'm serious about not expecting anything from you. If I hadn't married, I might have had this baby through a donor."

"Will Sergio's parents want to be involved, if it turns out to be his child?"

"Probably, and I'm not sure how I feel about that, although I've always liked both of them. I'm hoping his father wasn't involved in anything shady."

"That hotel has a pretty good reputation, but things aren't always what they appear to be."

"No, they're not." Her voice had a musing quality to it. Was she thinking about Sergio and wishing he'd survived? Although, under the circumstances, he couldn't see her staying married if what he'd read about the man was true. "Things could be much simpler if…"

Her voice faded away, maybe forgetting whom she was talking to. Because he could have sworn she'd been about to say that things would have been much simpler if the baby was Diego's rather than Sergio's. Ha! Simpler for her, but definitely not for him. Or her baby.

She took a deep breath and shook her head. "I guess we should be getting back. You have an early day tomorrow, right?"

"I do. Don't you as well?"

"No, I'm on call in case they need me, but I'm planning to go look at that house again. The one I told you about."

"Oh, right. Right. Let me know how it is."

"I'm going to try to take some pictures. It'll be good to have a place of our own."

For a second he froze, then realized she was talking about her and the baby. Not her and Diego.

She moved to go and stumbled, dropping her purse, which tumbled down several of the steps. He gripped her elbow. "Are you okay?"

"Yes, just a klutz."

He smiled. "You are anything but." He jogged down the steps and retrieved the item, coming back and handing it to her.

"Thank you."

"You're welcome." A quick snatch of something went through his mind. A snapshot of Bree, well into her pregnancy, her long hair flowing around her shoulders as she gripped his elbow as they made their way down these very same steps. Something burned in his throat, something he tried to will away, even as they trekked down the shallow stairs until they reached the parking area.

She slid into the passenger seat and waited for him to get in and start the vehicle. "How are the roads at night?"

"They're pretty good. Although, when the A19 was shut down a few months ago, it took a lot longer to get from Palermo to Catania because of the mountains and winding roadways."

"It's probably a nice drive, though."

"It is. Especially if you want to get off the beaten path."

She laughed, and he glanced at her. "What?"

"I don't know. Just something about that struck me as funny. I think I'm off the beaten track right now. I've exited the highway and am going through some pretty rocky terrain."

He smiled, despite himself, feeling a camaraderie with her that he didn't expect. "I think we both are."

"I really am sorry, Diego. If only I hadn't stopped in that bar…"

"I stopped in there, too. We both made the same choices. Made the same mistakes."

"Mistakes." Her voice was low and sad.

"I don't want this baby to ever think he or she was a mistake."

Merda. That wasn't what he'd meant to say.

"I phrased that badly." He glanced over to see her hands gripped tightly together.

"No, you said exactly what I was thinking. But I want to change that. At least on my part. I want to give this baby the best parts of me."

That was just it. The best parts of Diego were related to his job. It was the one thing he knew he was good at. And he'd poured himself into that at the cost of everything else.

Just like his father had.

And just like his dad, he was terrible at relationships. Terrible at spending time outside the hospital on anything except sleeping and showering. Even his friendships were mainly formed around people he worked with. Going to the bar that night by himself had been out of character for him. His relationships were always pretty clear-cut. And he chose women whose end goals were the same as his—as in nonexistent. So when Selina had mentioned children, it had ended the relationship. Maybe she'd hoped she could change him. But Diego hadn't wanted to change. At least, not at that moment.

Because he knew—*knew!*—the truth about himself, even if the world at large hadn't guessed. It's why he'd had that dragon emblazoned on his arm after the breakup of his first relationship, as a reminder to himself that his nature was not what most women were looking for. Tangle with him and you were apt to come out on the losing side emotionally.

Bree, on the other hand, was the polar opposite of him.

"You're going to make a very good mother."

She looked at him but didn't say anything for a minute. Didn't give him any empty assurances that he would make a great dad as well. Because he hadn't even said whether he'd be willing to be a father to this child.

"I hope so. I'm pretty scared, actually."

There was a raw vulnerability in her tone that pulled at something inside him. He wished he could say something profound that would help her feel less afraid, but there was nothing. Because the thought of actually becoming a dad was…terrifying. To be in the very same position his dad had been when he'd been born and stand there and… decide if this tiny human would get some of his time—or not. He wanted to be the kind of person who could make those sacrifices with gladness, but in some ways he didn't know who he was outside work. Was that how his father had felt, too? That gnawing uncertainty of who he really was?

He reached over and gripped her hand, his thumb brushing over her skin. "I'm sorry, Bree. I can't even imagine." He couldn't. He was having trouble grasping what was happening right now. If his response could be what it needed to be. And it was tearing something inside him into tiny pieces. Pieces he wasn't sure could be reassembled.

He wanted to be the kind of man his child could be proud of but, was he that man? Oh, he was good at his job. Very good. But he didn't know if he was a good person.

He hoped so. But until he was sure… Did he have a right to play a pivotal role in this child's life?

He didn't know. And that fact was giving him a whole boatload of regret. So he said the only thing he could think of. The only thing that was true.

"I'm scared, too."

A day later Bree sat at her perfusion table on what was supposed to have been her day off watching as Diego worked his magic on yet another heart. With steady hands and a determined jaw, it was hard to equate the man he was this morning with the one who'd admitted to being scared.

He'd never seemed more confident than he did right now. But then again, this room was a place in which he felt at home, a place where he knew his way around.

But to wrap his head around being a father? Yes, she could see how that might seem pretty terrifying.

She was scared, too. And strangely, his admission was he first time she'd felt a real emotional tether to him. Oh, he was sexy and the things he'd done to her that night at the bar had been surreal. But the softer side?

Honestly, saying he was scared was the first time she'd seen that softness. Or even believed there might be something more to him than a brilliant heart surgeon and a gifted lover.

"How are we doing?"

His words yanked her thoughts back to the task at hand. Only unlike her first surgery with him, she knew he wasn't using the word *we* to mean him and her. It was about their time clock. And it was her job to know how long the patient had been on bypass down to the minute.

"Two hours, eleven minutes on bypass."

His eyes met hers for a moment. And she was right. There was no fear there. No emotion whatsoever except a steely determination that was contagious. His team fed off his energy, and it was kind of amazing to watch. Even Bree, who considered herself pretty self-contained and separate from the actual surgical team, got caught up in that energy.

He set the world around him on fire. Just like that fire-breathing dragon inked on his arm. Maybe that's what it represented. That fiery energy that consumed everything in its path. She just had to be careful that it didn't consume her, too.

He was asking for some specialized tool,

and since her board had been Steady Eddie this whole time, she took a few seconds to study him, trying to figure out what it was about him that was so captivating.

The individual pieces of Diego's face could tempt a sculptor, but there were some slight imperfections that made the overall package come across as rugged and sexy rather than pretty. She couldn't quite put her finger on what it was, though. It wasn't his crooked smile that lifted higher on the left than on the right. Or his nose that had a slight bump on the bridge. Or his hair, which could be sleek and tame or wild with riotous waves.

Unpredictable. That's what the man was. It wasn't just his physical presence that overwhelmed her, but his nature. He could morph from a colleague into a fierce boss in the space of a few seconds, one that demanded that jobs were done well, including by him.

He glanced up again and caught her staring. "Something wrong?"

Fire licked at her face, and she could have sworn that tattoo under his sleeve was glowing with heat, ready to spew its flames in her direction.

She swallowed. "No, I just wondered how things were going."

One brow went up, but he didn't challenge her. He'd caught her and they both knew it. "It's going *meravigliosamente*."

Marvelously. Her blush deepened. She was pretty sure, judging from a couple of chuckles from the people around him, that adverb wasn't one he normally used.

But at least he'd seemed amused rather than angry. But it wouldn't do to let her attention wander again.

She gave a quick nod and this time focused on the readings in front of her until Diego needed her to do something else. Which he did around forty minutes later, when he was ready to wean the patient off her machine.

The switch from bypass back to the patient's own heart went without a hitch. It was as if Diego had written the book on every heart surgery in existence and excelled at them all. She was sure that wasn't the case, but right now it seemed that way.

She was in awe of his skill.

I'm scared, too.

She could not picture this man saying that. Not about a surgery. Not about much of anything.

"Preparing to close up."

For Diego, the exciting part of surgery had to be over, kind of like when she turned the patient's circulation back over to the team. But if so, you couldn't tell it by the meticulous way he wired the sternum back together. By the small, even stitches that she'd seen on every patient she'd worked on with him. Not that there'd been all that many. But each one told a story. That there wasn't any one part of the surgery that was more important than another. It all mattered.

Diego asked for a different type of suture once he'd finished stitching the muscles together. He was preparing for the final step: closing the skin. It was funny how even though Bree didn't have a clear view of what was happening from where she sat, she could still tell exactly what Diego was doing. Not just by his running commentary, but by the instruments he asked for. From scalpels to cauterizers to sponges, each part had its own special place in the process. Just like every person did.

And he was good at letting people know that. At making them feel special and needed.

She'd felt it that night at the bar. But she hadn't been looking for special or needed that night. She was looking for something that would numb her pain. Instead of numbing it, however, Diego had brought an ecstasy that had accomplished the same thing. But the next morning they both went their separate ways, and there'd been nothing to make her think they would ever see each other again.

Ha! She glanced up again, making sure she didn't pause too long this time. Who would have ever thought she'd be sitting in an operating room working less than fifteen feet from that very same man?

Certainly not her.

The snip of scissors sounded, as if putting a period on the act of surgery.

He instructed the surgical nurse on how he wanted the site dressed and which medications were to be administered when. The nurse charted everything on her tablet and read the instructions back to him.

"Yes, that's correct."

Diego glanced around the room in that way he did, his gaze touching each person present, including her.

Heat surged into her face all over again. There was no good reason for it. The man just affected her in ways that she'd rather he didn't. But hopefully he wasn't aware of it.

"All right. I think we're about done here. Any comments? Suggestions?"

His eyes skated over the room again. "No? Well, good job everyone. Signor Moseli's bypass should give him quite a few more years. I appreciate you coming in on a weekend."

Several people murmured that they didn't mind. Bree bet they didn't. Who wouldn't want to work with the renowned surgeon?

Regardless of her personal issues with Diego, she was smart enough to know that she could learn a lot from the man. And that this was a great opportunity. She just had to be careful not to let her emotions run rampant and turn her into some kind of fangirl. She was pretty sure he wouldn't appreciate or welcome that kind of fawning. Not that she would. She didn't normally wear her heart on her sleeve. But that didn't mean that things couldn't affect it. They could. So she would be cautious about opening up around him.

"I hope everyone has good rest of their weekend. I'll try not to drag you down here again. See you all again on Monday."

Diego smiled, and when he did, it seemed to be aimed right at her, even though she was sure that it probably wasn't.

But heaven help her, even after swearing she wouldn't fawn over him, she couldn't stop what happened next: she smiled back.

CHAPTER SIX

ETNA WAS BEING a naughty girl today.

A deep plume of smoke was roiling from the top of her, making it almost impossible to see the mountain peak.

Diego was knocking at her door first thing Tuesday morning. "Are you sure you want to do this today?"

She motioned him in. "I'm fine with going. If you think it's too dangerous, we can always just go partway up."

"It's not that it's dangerous. The visibility just won't be very good. And it'll be worse the higher we go, and the air quality will go down." He moved into the space. "How did your house looking go?"

"Great. I think the one I told you about is the one I'm going to get. I put a deposit on it and took some pictures. Do you want to see?" She wasn't sure why she was so excited, but she was. Maybe because she'd barely seen Diego since their trip to Palermo. The trip where he'd admitted to being scared, too. That admission had moved her in a way she hadn't expected. And she'd hoped to run into him at the hospital, just to see him.

And boy, was the guy a hunk today in a short-sleeved brown polo and a pair of cargo shorts. His legs were very masculine, with a light dusting of hair and a deep tan that said he spent time in the sun, although she'd heard he didn't have much of a social life. At least not that the people at the hospital knew of.

Not that she tried to pump people for information. But whenever his name came up somewhere in conversation, she found her ears immediately pricking, even when she didn't want to listen. He was an enigma, even to those who'd worked with him for years, it seemed.

He sat on the futon with her, and she immediately realized that was a mistake. His shampoo or aftershave or whatever it was smelled amazingly delicious. Or maybe it was just him. But it was distracting, and she found herself fumbling with her phone, trying to find the pictures while acting as nonchalant as she could—not an easy feat. Especially with the bottom edge of his tattoo peeking from below the sleeve of his shirt. She knew exactly was inked there. She'd actually kissed it, running her lips over the lines of it.

There! Finally!

She scrolled through the pictures, answering his questions and trying her best not to move deeper into his personal space.

"What's that?"

She glanced at the screen. "It's the balcony off the bedroom."

"Nice. It's very private." His words were low. Husky. "Just like the one at your hotel room."

Her belly quivered in response. Until he added, "You'll be sitting out there with a book and a cup of coffee before you know it."

Squelch. That's not what she'd been picturing doing out on that balcony. She hurriedly moved to the next picture, which was...the bedroom. Ack!

"Does it come furnished?" he asked.

"Yes, everything in it stays, which is a good thing, since I don't have any furniture of my own."

Two more pictures and they were done. Finally! She stood up, trying to make it look as casual as possible. He did not need to know that her knees were shaking and her head felt slightly off-kilter. As did her heart, which had begun pounding when he'd mentioned how private her balcony was. She was going to have a hard time getting those words out of her head.

"I made a lunch. I wasn't sure what they have up there in the way of food." She motioned to the backpack sitting on the table. "I put it in there in case we were going to hike up the mountain."

He walked over and slung the rucksack onto one shoulder with ease, despite the fact that it had a couple of liters of water stuffed in there as well as sandwiches and some fruit. "Thanks. I have some water in the car as well. There are spots to park as you go up, so we can get out and move around and decide how much of it we want to walk."

"I know we're planning on talking about

things, but thanks for offering to do it on the mountain. It's really the one place I wanted to see while in Sicily."

"While in Sicily? Are you not planning to stay here?"

She blinked. "Well, I'm not assuming I'll be moving anytime soon, but you never know what the future holds."

"I see." But she didn't really think he did, because his brows had come together in a way that suggested he wasn't happy about something she'd said. It was about moving. And his reaction was exactly what she thought it might be, since he'd once said he couldn't imagine himself living anywhere but Catania.

But if he, for some reason, decided he didn't want to be a part of the baby's life, what did it matter where she lived? And she might want to be closer to her mom and dad, if that were the case.

Her mouth tightened. He couldn't have it both ways. He was either all in…or he was out. Completely out. Her father had been there for her for every step of her life. Ballet recitals. Graduations. And in the most heart-breaking time of her life, he'd been right there to pick up the pieces. She couldn't imagine anything less for her child. She wouldn't *allow* for anything less. "We can talk about that, too. We each have plans for the future. I'd like to know what yours are."

"My plans are to remain here in Sicily."

There'd been no softening of his gaze, but there had been a weird strangled sound to the words. As if they'd been forced out of him against his will. So if he decided he wanted to be a part of the baby's life and she eventually needed to move for a new job opportunity, was he saying he wouldn't come?

"My plans for the moment are to do the same, but circumstances don't always allow us to do what we want."

"Yes. I know."

Great. They were not getting off to the best start. Maybe a change of scenery would help. "Are you ready? Maybe we should go while the weather is still nice."

Thankfully, he agreed immediately, probably feeling the same uncomfortable tension that she had. Diego carried the backpack and a quilt she wanted to bring and loaded them into the back seat of the car.

Then he started the vehicle, put it into Drive, and they were off.

She might move? That thought had not even crossed Diego's mind. But it should have. She hadn't been born in Sicily—in fact, her family was in Naples, and she probably had other family in the States. Why would he think that she would stay here forever?

Maybe because she might be having his baby.

Except Diego was still wrestling with the ramifications of that. Bree's words had made him realize that being involved with his child might prove to be complicated. There could be decisions—hard decisions—on top of the main one in question: How hard was it going to be for him to change his ways? To give time that he'd never learned to give?

The drive up the first quarter of the mountain was done in silence. Until he heard Bree gasp and, looking over at her, saw that she was staring out over the terrain. Right before the road curved to the left, it looked like the mountain peaks had lined up, going from short to tallest. He relaxed. She said she loved Sicily. The longer she was here, the more likely it was to grow on her.

And the more she would grow on him. He could feel it happening already.

And if this baby *wasn't* his? He wasn't positive he could back away from her the way he'd once thought he could.

And that scared the hell out of him.

So was he hoping the child was his?

For once he allowed himself to relax. To forget about everything but being up here with her. "It's amazing, yes?"

"Yes. I don't think I've ever seen anything like it. And the smoke seems to have dissipated, or maybe it's just blowing in another direction."

"That happens sometimes. I'm glad we're able to see. There will be a spot to pull over in about a half a mile. Do you want to do some walking? Or…" His gaze ventured to her stomach, which was still flat. For a second he imagined what it would look like in six months' time, with a cute little bulge where their baby was growing and a—

Their baby?

"I'd like to walk. It's still cool outside, and

my sandals are comfortable. I can carry the backpack, if you want."

"I'll carry it." He sent her a smile, hoping that didn't sound chauvinistic.

They got to the stopping place. They weren't the only ones who were going to do some exploring. There were several other cars here as well, and a few people milling around the area.

He parked and got out and grabbed the pack while Bree hesitated. "How long are we going to be out? Do you want me to bring the quilt?"

"I thought we might come back to the car and go up farther. There's a pretty overlook where we can set up everything. I just thought we might want some water. I also brought a cooler and some ice."

"That sounds great. Thanks."

Maybe by the time they got to their ultimate destination, he would have figured out how to explain what his thoughts were. He figured she didn't want a testing period. She wanted a black-or-white, yes-or-no answer. But what about a compromise that tested the waters before the baby was actually born? Maybe he could put himself on trial and let

Bree give him a verdict on his performance. If he couldn't make himself better than his father, then she had the right to say no to him being involved.

He had to be careful how he worded it, because it would be easy for her to take it the wrong way and cut him off without giving him a chance. He'd kind of done that to himself, hadn't he? Cut himself off by deciding not to have kids.

And now fate had laughed that decision into the dust and set him on a path there seemed to be no coming back from.

They hiked over to an area that allowed them to see off into the distance. Her pink denim backpack was smaller than the one he normally carried, so slinging it over one shoulder had been his best bet. But it worked.

And he liked shouldering a tiny portion of her burden. It wasn't a baby, but spending time with a woman like this was out of his norm. This took a lot more time than just falling into bed with someone and fixing them breakfast the next morning before heading back to work—like he'd done in recent years. This required a lot more...effort.

And he didn't resent it. In fact, he'd looked forward to today. It was a tiny step, and God only knew if it was sustainable for him in the long haul. But he wanted to try.

"How far up the mountain can we go?"

"We can drive up to about the two-thousand-meter point. To actually hike to the top, we'd have to be part of a group headed by a professional tour guide. They have safety equipment and climbing gear in case of an accident. I didn't think to reserve a spot—sorry about that."

"It's fine. I just wondered." She glanced out over the mountainside before tilting her head. She held a hand to her brows to shade her line of vision. "What's that?"

"Where?"

"That black ridge. There's not much growing on it."

He glanced out to see what she was looking at. "That's a lava field."

She blinked. "As in real lava?"

That made him smile. "Yep. Produced the natural way, by a volcano. I don't think they're interested in manufacturing lava just for tourists."

"Ha! Okay, I guess that wasn't the brightest question. It just surprised me. Can I touch it?"

"I don't see why not." He'd just started to move that way when they heard someone scream and then cry out in pain.

Bree whipped around, looking for whoever had made the distressed sound. "There! Someone's on the ground."

They made their way closer, only to have someone motion them back. "There's a snake."

"Venomous?"

"I think so, judging by the head," said the man. "I'm pretty sure it's an asp viper."

Asp vipers were the only venomous snakes in the area.

Bree slid past the man. "We're medical professionals."

"Be careful. Please," the concerned man said. "We don't need anyone else getting hurt."

A young woman dressed in shorts and a T-shirt lay on the ground staring at something. Her hands were wrapped around her lower leg.

He spotted it. A beige snake with black markings and the familiar anvil-shaped head of a viper lay about twenty feet away. It looked like the victim had scooted back from it, but the snake was still coiled and looked ready to strike again. But at that distance it wouldn't be able to reach her.

Diego put a hand on Bree's shoulder. "Let me find a stick."

"The hell with that." Before he could stop her, she removed one of her sandals and went over to stand right beside the victim, then she cranked her arm back and let the shoe fly. It slammed into the ground near the snake hard enough to send dirt flying in all directions. Evidently the reptile decided it had had enough excitement for the day, because it slithered through a rocky pass, disappearing from view.

She knelt beside the woman. "Let me see your leg. Diego is a doctor, and I'm a Perfusionist. What's your name?"

"Oh my God. Thank you. I think you saved my life. I'm Lydia." She took her hands off her leg, where blood trickled freely. There were twin marks that definitely looked to be caused by fangs. Then Bree turned her attention to Diego. "What type of venom do they have?"

He heard her question but was already phoning in, asking that an EMS squad be sent to their location. They were about twenty minutes out. Until then they would have to do first aid and pray that the snake didn't decide to pay them another visit. Bree had saved some valuable time by tossing that shoe. But it was also a risk. One she'd been willing to take when no one else had. "Asp viper venom is a hemotoxin," he said. "It affects the clotting system."

He crouched down with her and zipped open her backpack. "Do you have something in here I can use as a tourniquet?" They needed to at least slow the flow of venom to other parts of her body.

"No, but I have this." She stood up and took off the belt around her waist and handed it to him.

"Perfect." He wrapped the slim band of leather twice around the woman's thigh and buckled it in place.

The woman pressed a hand to her mouth and moaned. "It's starting to really hurt."

"I know. Are you here with anyone?"

She shook her head, tears coming to her eyes. "No. I broke up with my boyfriend last week and decided to come on vacation anyway to get back at him. We already had reservations here."

He saw Bree's teeth come down on her lip. Maybe thinking of her own reasons for originally coming to Sicily.

"Is it supposed to hurt this much?"

At first, he thought she was talking about the breakup, then realized she mean the pain in her leg.

His own breakup as a young medical student had been devastating and had sent him spinning into an orbit from which he'd never returned. And hadn't wanted to.

Until now?

He pulled his mind back to the work at hand.

The venom was already causing damage. Soon some of the tissue would start turning dark as mini hemorrhages began to erupt near the site of the bite, spreading as the toxin moved through the limb.

Bree took the woman's vitals. "It's important to stay calm, Lydia, even though I know it's the hardest thing you've ever done."

Diego had to admit that looking down the barrel of a pregnancy was one of the hardest things he'd ever done. But it wasn't death. Or the possible loss of a limb. And if this woman could sit here and not be a screaming wreck, then he could damn well face the toxin of his own past and stay calm, working on it until he found the right treatment.

Bree wrapped her arm around the woman's shoulders. "Emergency services will be here soon to take you to the hospital."

Her eyes widened. "Am I going to die? I need to call my boyfriend. Well, my exboyfriend."

"No. You're not going to die." Bree said it softly but firmly as Diego kept track of the time on the tourniquet. It would have to be loosened periodically so that blood flow was not completely interrupted from her leg. "You can call him later. Once you're feeling better."

Five minutes later they heard the sound of a siren coming up the mountain road.

The perfusionist gave Lydia a squeeze. "See? What did I tell you? They'll take you to get some antivenin. It'll counteract the snake's venom."

Lydia moaned again, trying to look down

at her leg. "I had no idea there were snakes in Italy."

Diego glanced at her. "You're not from Italy?"

"No." She sucked down a deep breath. "My parents are Italian, but I was born in Switzerland. It's where my boyfriend and I live. It's always been my dream to come to Sicily."

He patted her arm. "Don't let this change that. We really are a pretty nice lot." He nodded in the direction the snake had gone. "Most of us, anyway."

The woman actually laughed, and Bree smiled her approval at him. His insides turned to quicksand, trapping him in an impossible grip. He stared at her for several seconds as her smile continued to shine.

Dios, he would make every person in the near vicinity laugh if it would get her to look at him like that again. It was like at the bar where they'd first met. She'd turned and smiled at him, and it was as if something in those upturned lips and dimple had bewitched him, causing him to act in ways he might not ordinarily have. He'd never picked up a woman in a bar before. Ever. And from the sound of it, neither had Bree. Two people acting out of character and look what had happened. A baby.

His baby.

He clenched his teeth. No, it would only be his child if Bree determined he was good enough. The last thing he wanted was to be like his own father and make a mess of his child's life. He'd once heard his mother arguing with his dad, saying that all he was was a sperm donor. Diego had been young at the time and had gone to his ten-year-old brother and asked him what those strange words meant.

All his brother had said was that it meant his father wasn't really their father. Diego had taken that literally until he was old enough to work out what Antonio had meant.

He did not want to be a father who wasn't really a father. So if he wanted to change things, he was going to have to work damn hard to prove to Bree—and himself—that he could.

Someone motioned the pair of EMS workers over to them. They were carrying a portable gurney with them. Diego quickly filled them in.

"Where's the snake now?"

"He's gone, but several of us saw it. It was a *Vipera aspis* for sure." He glanced at his watch. "It's been three minutes since the tourniquet was last loosened. It was put on a total of seven minutes ago."

The man looked at him, eyes wide. "You're a medical worker?"

Yeah, it might have been nice if he'd identified himself first thing. "I'm a cardiac surgeon." He motioned to Bree. "She's in medicine as well."

"Well, thanks for making our job easier by not trying to suck out the venom."

Diego smiled. "No worries there."

They got the woman loaded up, who despite the pain flaring across her face had reached for Bree. The perfusionist took her hand and squeezed it. "Go and feel better. I'll come by the hospital later and see how you're doing." She glanced at the EMTs. "Where are you taking her?"

"Concepción."

"Perfect, that's our hospital. They're very good at what they do. We'll meet you there."

So Bree had gone from checking on Lydia later to meeting her at the hospital. He had a feeling it had something to do with the breakup. Maybe she really was comparing it to what she'd gone through.

Evidently that ended their trip up Etna. But that was okay, because he still had no idea what he was going to say to her.

Diego watched them load the frightened woman up. "I take it we're abandoning our trip."

"I think it's for the best. I really do want to see how she's doing. Besides…" She wiggled the toes of her right foot. "I don't think I'm going to want to hike around with one shoe on and one shoe off."

The shoe had skipped to the edge of a downward slope. "I'll go get—"

"No." She shuddered. "I'm actually terrified of snakes. I don't want to take the chance of it being over that ridge somewhere watching. And I don't think I can ever wear that shoe again, knowing where it's been."

Said as if it was somehow contaminated. "I'll tell you what. I'll get you to the car, and then I'll come back for the shoe." When she acted like she was going to argue, he shook his head. "You don't have to wear it again.

I'll put it in a bag and throw it away, but we can't leave it there."

She shut her eyes. "I know. I just don't want it near me."

"It won't be. You never have to look at it again." He turned his back to her. "Hop on."

There was silence behind him. He turned his head to look.

Her mouth was open, and she looked shocked. "Excuse me?"

"You can ride on my back. How do you say it in English?"

"A piggyback ride? I don't think so. I can walk."

He glanced at the terrain, which was strewn with pebbles, some of them sharp black volcanic rock. "Your feet will be cut to pieces before you've gone ten feet. And we've already walked a couple hundred yards." He grinned at her. "Unless you'd like me to throw you over my shoulder like a *pompiere* would do." He reached down and picked up her backpack and the quilt, holding them in one hand, the other arm ready to do exactly what he'd said.

"But you're not a fireman." She took a deep breath, looking at the ground. "Okay.

I'll get on, but don't you tell *anyone* about this."

"I won't. Promise." Even if she hadn't made him promise, there was no way he was going back to the hospital and telling everyone within hearing distance that he'd carted Bree around on his back.

He felt her hands go to his shoulders, and she leaped, her legs wrapping around his hips in a way that made things shift and then…tighten. His free arm scooped under one of her bare legs to hold her in place before realizing they weren't going to make it without him holding on to her better. "Can you take the quilt? Drape it around my neck or something."

Somehow, she managed to take the cover and lay it over his shoulder, along with the strap of the backpack. Then, wrapping his arms beneath both of her legs, he started back down the hill.

CHAPTER SEVEN

OH, GOD, WHY did you have to wear a skirt today of all days?

With her arms wrapped around his neck, trying to make sure her forearm was holding the quilt in place, there was no way to rescue the hem of her skirt, which was riding higher and higher on her thighs. Thighs that were becoming sensitized by rubbing against his lean hips. She could hear him breathing from the exertion of going down some of the steeper parts of the hill, and one time his foot slid on some loose gravel and she closed her eyes, expecting to crash to the ground. But she didn't. He'd righted himself and kept on walking.

"I should have let you find a stick."

"I don't think I could hold a walking stick."

She shook her head, even though she knew he couldn't see her. "I mean a stick to throw at the snake."

"No," Several more steps. "You did the right thing."

"Why don't you stop and take a rest?"

His head swiveled from right to left as he shook it to mean no. "If I put you down, I know you well enough to know you'll never get up again. Not that much farther."

He was right. There was no way she'd make him carry her again. If she'd realized how far they'd come, she'd have never agreed to this stupid plan in the first place. But here she was. And he was still going back for the shoe afterward.

Why hadn't she just let him pick it up? Thinking about it, she'd probably sounded extremely childish, saying she wouldn't wear the shoe. But she had a phobia of snakes. She didn't know what had possessed her to try to scare the thing away anyway. Maybe because she'd pictured Diego picking up some kind of stick and getting close enough to its fangs to get bitten, too. If it had come toward them, would she have stood her ground? Or abandoned her patient? Thank heaven she hadn't had to make that choice.

"I'm sorry, Diego. It was stupid of me to leave my shoe behind."

He gave a chuckle. "I'm rather enjoying this."

His breathing didn't quite sound like he was enjoying it. Then again, her breathing wasn't exactly steady, either, but there was a completely different reason for that. With his arms looped under her legs, it was as if he were holding her in place—holding her tightly against his body. If he'd been facing her rather than having his back to her... Her thighs rubbed again, and sensation arced with lightning speed to the area he would have been touching. Oh, man, it didn't bear thinking about.

She tried to pull air in and out of her lungs in slow deep breaths, but her brain had already shifted onto another track. She wasn't going to survive this.

Even now her nipples were tightening, every jostle of his body providing a delicious friction that made her want to whimper and press closer. Instead she tried to lean slightly back to take the pressure off.

"Hey, what are you doing back there?" His voice had a gurgling quality to it. "You're choking me."

"Sorry!" She pressed against him again, loosening her grip on his neck.

Scrape, scrape went her thighs. And her blouse against her sensitive nipples. Every footfall he made just upped the ante. And now that central area between her thighs was beginning a familiar tingle that spelled disaster.

They came upon another couple who were walking in the opposite direction. The man was on his phone. He looked at them twice, eyes going wide. Before she could say anything, Diego said, "Missing shoe. It's a long story."

"You're that woman who threw her shoe at the snake, aren't you?"

"I—I…" She couldn't think of a thing to say.

As the couple passed them, the woman smiled at her. "Well done. I don't think I would have been courageous enough to do that."

Thankfully they had already passed them

by the time her tongue was able to free itself from the roof of her mouth.

Oh, God, the car. She saw it! If she could just survive another fifteen feet, she would soon be...

They got to the hood of the sports car, and she took the quilt from his shoulder and tossed it onto the vehicle. "You can put me down now." *Please, please put me down.*

Instead of letting her slide down, his arms tightened. "Are you sure that's what you want? For me to let go?"

Had he felt her reaction to him? Maybe she'd bored twin holes into his back.

"Yes. Thank you for carrying me, though."

Thankfully, he released her legs, and she scrambled down his body, doing her best to keep her skirt from riding all the way up. Once down, she made sure her arms were over her chest before he turned to face her.

He glanced at her face and then moved down to her crossed arms. When his eyes came back up, one side of his mouth twitched slightly.

Oh, hell. He knew. He *knew*! Her face heated to something that would rival Armageddon as she stood there. She was so tempted to look to see if there was any answering response on his part, but he would know exactly what she was doing if she did. And right now, she preferred to pretend she had no idea what he was thinking.

"You're very welcome. Anytime."

Not very likely. "I don't think I'll be throwing my shoe again."

He smiled. "Speaking of shoes. You'll be okay here while I go retrieve it?"

"Oh, Diego, first you have to carry me down the mountain, now you have to make that trip all over again."

"It's not a problem. Get in the car, and I'll turn the air on." He retrieved two of the water bottles from the cooler when he threw the quilt and backpack onto the back seat and handed her one of the bottles. The water was super cold and hit her system with a welcome jolt that would hopefully ice down some of her earlier thoughts.

He climbed in the driver's seat and cranked the engine, keeping the parking brake on while shifting the vehicle into Neutral. It didn't take long for the air to cool the space, drying the sweat on her and making a chill rush through her system. She couldn't suppress a shiver.

"Too much?"

"No, it's perfect."

"Okay, lock the door when I get out."

She nodded. "Please be careful. You don't know where that thing went."

"Will you come and throw your other shoe at it if it gets me, too?"

This time she laughed. "And how will you carry me back down the mountain if you're bitten, too?"

"I would find a way."

With those enigmatic words, he was gone, slamming the door and leaving her to stare after him. He would, too. Find a way. Or at least try to. He was that kind of man. So why was it so hard for him to commit to a child that he might have had a part in conceiving?

She could just as easily ask herself why it was so easy to expect him to, when he'd had no say in whether she kept the baby or terminated the pregnancy.

Why hadn't she considered that?

Because something inside her was already attached to this little bean—or whatever size the fetus currently was. She wanted it. And she didn't want Diego to feel like he needed to want it, too. Even though in her heart that's exactly what she was hoping. It was stupid. And it was selfish. And she needed to try to prepare herself for the reality that he really might not want to be a father. Who was she to dictate how he felt or didn't feel?

Maybe he would choose to walk away, just like Sergio had. God, she hoped not. She didn't know why, but she wasn't quite ready for him to be out of her life.

A half hour passed before he finally returned. But there was nothing in his hands. She frowned, waiting for him to climb inside. "What happened? Couldn't you find it?"

"I did." He looked at her. "Did you want it?"

"No. Where is it?"

"In a rubbish bin on the path. I can go back and get it if you've changed your mind."

"No, I definitely haven't. Thank you. I know it's stupid, I just—"

"You just can't stand looking at it every day and remembering its significance. I understand all too well."

Its significance? Was he thinking about

how, once she had this baby, he wouldn't be able to stand looking at him or her every day without remembering the child's significance? That he or she was conceived as the result of a stupid one-night stand? What had he called it?

A mistake.

A spear of pain went through her. Just like carrying her down that mountain, was she putting a burden on him that she had no right to make him bear? Maybe demanding he take part in raising this baby was wrong. Maybe it was downright cruel.

But what else could she do? She had to think of her baby, too.

I would find a way.

Wasn't that what he'd said? But carrying her down a mountain was different than taking on a lifetime commitment.

"Would you mind swinging by the hospital before you drop me off so I can check on Lydia?" She realized there was another answer. One that would make it easier on him. "Sorry, I guess there's no reason why you couldn't take me back to the hotel and let me drive over."

"I'd like to make sure she's okay, too, so

we'll go to the hospital first. That is, if you can stand being in the car with me a little while longer."

Had he guessed her thoughts from a few seconds ago? No, she was pretty sure he had no idea what she'd been mulling over, and she was glad. She had a lot to think about tonight.

"Of course I can. I do need a shoe, though. I don't think the hospital would approve of one of its employees traipsing around barefoot. If you could just find a store and let me run in on the way?"

The trip to the hospital seemed to take a lot less time than their trek down the mountain on foot. After a successful shoe mission, Diego found a spot and pulled the car into it. She wiggled her toes in her new jewel-encrusted flip-flops. It was all they'd had in her size.

They got out and headed up to the front entrance. "I didn't get her last name," she said.

"I'm pretty sure all we have to say is snake bite victim and they'll know where she is."

Diego went up to the information desk and took a minute to chitchat with the person manning the station before he came back. "She's not in ICU, so that's a good thing. She's on the third floor."

They went up the elevator, and she followed him down the hallway until they got to the room. Diego knocked, and a woman's voice called for them to enter.

Diego opened the door and held it so she could pass through it. Once they got inside, they saw Lydia sitting up in bed, the area around her ankle stained with a black permanent marker, showing the spread of damage over her leg. But the lines were close together, and it had been over an hour since the ambulance had left the scene.

Bree smiled at her. "You look remarkably well."

"They've given me some lovely painkillers." Her face contorted. "They said I was lucky. Very, very lucky. And I have you two to thank. The damage to my leg could have been so much worse. And it if had spread..."

Diego moved closer. "Emergency services were there in fifteen minutes. They had a lot to do with it."

"I'm just glad you were both there. Thank you. I truly mean that. If you hadn't acted quickly, who knows what might have happened."

Bree laid her palm on the woman's shoulder. "It looks like there's not much progression up your leg."

"No. Everyone was surprised. I might not even need another dose of whatever they used to counteract the poison."

It was a common mistake. Calling it poison rather than venom.

"I'm glad the antivenin is doing its job. Some of that depends on how much venom the snake injected. There's even such a thing as a dry bite, where no venom is released, although from your pain levels and the marks they've made on your leg, that wasn't the case this time."

Diego said, "Is there anything we can do? Anyone you'd like for us to call?"

She gave kind of a sheepish shrug. "I called Patrick—my boyfriend. He's trying to get a flight out right now."

She hadn't used the qualifier *ex* this time when she talked about him.

"That's wonderful," Bree said. She forced her voice to sound cheerful, even though she couldn't help but think of Sergio and wonder what would have happened if he'd chosen another path. If things had been different. They might have been starting their own family.

But they weren't. And now he was gone. Along with his deceit and lying.

She'd been thinking so much about Diego and his plans as far as the baby was concerned. But it might not even be his. She kept forgetting that one little fact. And if he wasn't, then all this angst she'd been going through—that she'd been putting Diego through—might all be for nothing. Because if the baby wasn't his, there was no way he was going to want anything to do with it. No way he would want anything to do with her. No chance…for anything.

Was that what she wanted? A chance for something? How did she know that Diego would stick around? That he was any more honest than Sergio had been?

He'd been honest about not wanting to be a father. He could have told her exactly what she wanted to hear and then skipped out. But he hadn't. And he was standing here right now. That was worth something, wasn't it?

She had no idea. And unfortunately it had

become kind of natural to think of him as the father. As somehow being in her life, even after such a short period of time. Was she fantasizing about things that would never happen?

Like she'd fantasized about him on the way down from that mountain?

Oh, yeah. She'd been on fire. For him.

The fantasy of spending one more night with the cardiac surgeon was going to be a hard one to banish. Because once she knew whose baby it was, one of two things was going to happen. He was either going to walk away with a huge sigh of relief, or he was going to stay because he had to.

He wasn't entirely immune to her, though. At least she didn't think he was.

So what would he say if she propositioned him to stay with her tonight? Would he think she was manipulating him in order to get him to stay in her life? Or would he take it at face value, as the request of a woman who desired a man? Physical desire. Not emotional.

God, at least she hoped it wasn't.

She glanced over at where he was talking to Lydia. As if sensing her eyes on him, he turned toward her. He blinked. Frowned. "Are you okay?"

"Yeah. I am, Diego. Really fine, actually."

He must have seen something in her face or heard it in her words, because that frown faded, and his head tilted as he studied her. Then a devastating half smile took its place. The same one he'd given her when he'd turned to look and saw her covering herself up with her arms.

Was she that easy to read?

He murmured to Lydia about how glad he was that she was feeling better and that someone was coming to be with her. That they'd check in on her again tomorrow.

They?

And that's when she knew. He was not only open to spending a few hours with her tonight. He might not be planning on going home at all.

Diego could have sworn he'd heard an invitation in Bree's voice a moment or two ago. But he waited until he got to the car before actually turning to look at her.

Disappointment sloshed through him. Whatever he'd seen was gone now. As if it had never been there at all. And maybe it hadn't. Maybe he'd imagined all of it.

"How are your new shoes feeling?"

"They're fine." She fiddled with the fabric of her skirt before looking at him again. "Hey…um, do you want to come up once we get to the hotel?"

Okay, so maybe it hadn't been wishful thinking after all.

"Yes, I would like that." Only this time, he didn't want to guess what she meant. He leaned forward so he could look at her. "Just to make sure…this isn't for coffee or tea… or to eat those sandwiches you made, as delicious as they might be, right?"

"I wasn't planning on offering you any of those things."

His brows went up as a whisper of anticipation crouched low in his belly. "And just what were you planning on offering me?"

She hesitated for a minute before placing her hand on his knee and squeezing. "Me."

The word was simple. Unadorned. And it moved him in a way not much could. In a way that nothing had in a very long time. Not with Angela. Not with Selina.

Without a word, he turned his key in the

ignition and backed out of the space before he was able to answer. "I accept your offer."

The trip to her hotel found the roads congested, just as they'd been on the trip into town. But this time there was an impatience in him that hadn't been there a half hour ago. The whole time he'd carried her down that hill, he'd been hyperaware of her weight on him, had remembered how it had felt to have her splayed across his hips in an entirely different way. And her breasts mashed against his back? That had been heaven. Sheer heaven. He'd had a hard time making it down without giving himself away. Had been out of breath and out of sorts, almost stumbling once as they continued their trip. He'd been glad to have to go back after her shoe, hoping it would give him time to compose himself before he had to face her again.

And he had done a decent job of it. Until she'd told him she had no intention of offering him coffee or sandwiches.

He'd be a fool to turn her down. Especially since both of their lives were about to change forever. This time there was no worry about pregnancy. Because Mother Nature had already taken care of that.

They could go back to his place—it was closer—but something kept him from going that route. She'd already inserted herself into his life—even though it hadn't been intentional—and he'd rather control the setting. And she'd already suggested her hotel. It was easier. Less personal. For both of them, since it wasn't a space either one of them would inhabit afterward. She had a place she was getting ready to move into. This event could just fade into both of their pasts, just like the previous hotel visit had done.

Except that hadn't faded into the past. Because Bree was here. And she was expecting his—or Sergio's—baby.

He decided to follow up on something. "It's okay? You're feeling okay?"

"Yes. I'm actually feeling better than I have in a couple of weeks."

He was glad. Not just because it meant they were going to sleep together again, but for her sake.

They got to her street, and Diego turned onto it. If he was going to back out, now was the time. Except he didn't want to. The other night he'd spent with her had been fantastic. Better than any night he'd ever spent with a woman. Something he really didn't want to examine too closely. Maybe that had been because at the time he knew there were no strings. No next-morning angst or regrets. Or at least he'd thought there'd been none.

But even that didn't deter him from wanting to be with her again, as evidenced by how fast he'd leaped at her offer. It was embarrassing, really. But that fact wasn't enough to make him want to back out. He didn't think anything would really make him want to do that. Unless she changed her mind.

Then they were out of the car and up the elevator, her hand clasped tightly in his as if he was afraid she would fly away if he let her go. He had a feeling it wasn't that. But more that he was trying to assure himself that this was true. That he wasn't dreaming this.

The second her front door swung shut behind them, he hauled her to him for a long kiss, eyes clenched tight as her remembered taste poured through him. Sweet. Like the sweetest wine. And the most potent tequila.

Her arms wound around his neck, and her breasts were again pressed tight against him.

And it was still heaven. He sighed, leaning back slightly to look at her. "I thought about this on the way down the mountain, you know."

"You did?" She smiled, that dimple hitting his gut and sliding down to the part of him that was already aching for her. "So did I. I was afraid you'd notice."

He decided to let her in on a little secret. "I did. But then I thought maybe I was imagining it. That I was just projecting my own thoughts onto you."

"Oh, there was no projecting going on at all." She grabbed his hand and started to lead him back to where he suspected her bedroom was, but he countered the move with one of his own.

"Let's save the bed." He looked at her. "For later."

She blinked at him.

Kissing her mouth again, he whispered. "I thought I saw a nice little balcony out there the last time I was here. The picture you showed me of your new place has one that's similar. Just as private."

Her breath washed across his mouth. "I like the way you think." She bit her lip. "I do have neighbors on either side of me, though. They can't see, but…"

They could hear. He caught her meaning. His cheek brushed against hers as he moved over to her ear. "We'll have to be very, very quiet, then. Can you do that?"

He didn't think she'd been the noisemaker the last time they were together. That had been all him. But the thought of trying to contain himself—to pour all his energy into loving her—was a heady thought. One he was pretty sure he could do, but that tiny hint of doubt…of having to purposely restrain himself from yelling out… It was a huge turn-on.

"Yes." Her whispered confirmation was all he needed to grab her to him with a growl and kiss her the way he'd been dying to all the way down that mountain.

She giggled. "I thought we were supposed to be quiet."

"Oh, believe me, I can be perfectly silent." His tongue touched her lower lip. "Perfectly. Still."

The shiver he felt against his chest hadn't been his imagination.

He scooped her up in his arms and carried her over to French doors that opened onto the outside space. Bree reached down and twisted the handle of the one to the right and pushed it away from them. With her still in his arms, he went through them, setting her down next to the railing, where walls extended out past the barrier, ensuring that no one on either side of them could see anything. And in front of them was nothing but the mountain.

CHAPTER EIGHT

BREE COULDN'T BELIEVE this was happening. And yet it was.

Diego was behind her, arms wrapped around her waist, his lips slowly brushing across the sensitive flesh of her neck. The sensation was slightly tickly, mixed with a whole lot of sensuality. This time there was no mistaking his reaction to being close to her. No need for her to look. She could feel him pressed tight against the top of her butt. She swallowed. She wanted to bend at the waist and let him slide her skirt up her legs, up her thighs…over the curve of her bottom. Her teeth sank into her lower lip as she struggled to contain a whimper that rose in her throat as she thought about what he was going to do to her. What she was going to do to him.

No sounds. She tried picturing her neighbors sitting on the other side of that partition enjoying their demitasses of Italian coffee.

Italian coffee. Pah! There was no comparison to the Italian she was currently enjoying.

His hands slid up to cup her breasts through her blouse before sliding down and with deliberate motions tugging the shirt up and over her head. There was no one in front of them to see, except for the mountain, and Bree was pretty sure Etna wouldn't be sharing anything that she saw.

Even so, she felt very naughty standing there in her bra. Then, that, too, suddenly went loose, the straps carrying the entire garment down her arms before dropping to the ground.

But she didn't have time to debate what to do, because no sooner had the slight breeze washed over her bare skin, causing her nipples to contract, than his hands covered her again, the warmth of his palms rivaling the heat of the outside air.

He nipped her ear, fingers moving from her breasts down the bare skin of her torso before finding her hips. He pulled her back against him, the hard ridge behind her making her gasp.

"Shh…"

Lord, she wanted to reach behind her and grip the backs of his thighs and keep him right where he was, but she'd have to let go of the railing to do that.

Then the very thing she'd fantasized about began to happen. Her skirt began inching up her legs.

Diego whispered in her ear, the Italian low and raw. *"Voglio te."*

He wanted her. Well, that wanting was mutual, only hers was wild and desperate. At this point, it couldn't happen fast enough. The anticipation had been building ever since the trip down the mountain, and she was pretty sure the second he touched her, she was going to explode. She squirmed against him, wishing he would hurry. Not because she was afraid someone would discover what they were doing, but because she needed to feel him again. Wanted that intimacy that only sex could bring.

And it was sex, right?

Nothing more.

Don't think about it, Bree.

So she didn't. Instead, she allowed herself to revel in the little things. The sound that her skirt made as it continued its whispered ascent. The breeze as it rustled the leaves of the plants that surrounded the space. The way her heart pounded in her chest.

Then her skirt was around her waist. She wasn't sure why he hadn't pushed it down her legs, but she didn't care. This was just as sexy. Maybe more so, since she now caught the sound of his zipper as the tab snicked across each tooth, separating them.

One hand cupped her chin and tipped her face to look at him before he kissed her deeply, his tongue filling her mouth. Her nerve endings went wild as she closed her lips around him, holding him in place before she felt him slide free.

Down went her panties, and his hands were back on her hips, tugging slightly to encourage her to take a step or two back. She took the opportunity to step out of her underwear as well.

She was tipped forward, exactly the way she'd imagined it. The sound of a packet being ripped open distracted her for a second before she shook off the sensation. Of course he would protect himself. Sergio had had who knew how many partners? But still there was a frisson of disappointment that she would not get to feel him skin to skin.

But it was okay. It was more than okay. He was still here with her.

And when she felt the touch of him against her, her eyes shut and she savored the sensation of him entering her, stretching her. His shaky breath blew across her ear. "I'm trying."

She had no idea what he was trying to do. To be quiet? To hold on?

Diego set a slow, languorous pace that made her squirm. And then his hand reached around to cup her, fingers touching sensitive places that sent her reeling toward madness.

She wanted to tell him to go faster, to push deeper, but she'd taken a vow of silence. So she tried to tell him with her body, pushing back against him with each thrust of his hips, arching into his hand to deepen the pressure there.

He got it. He wrapped his free arm around her waist and jerked her back to him, changing the pace inside her, increasing the friction in front.

Her nerve endings became a mass of activity, each electrical signal trying to catch her attention. And they did, quickly overloading her senses. The rush to the top happened with a speed that robbed her of breath, stole her thoughts. All she could do ride high and let the vortex overtake her. She exploded around him, somehow managing not to scream or moan or do any of the other things her body yelled for her to do.

His movements matched hers, and when he thrust deep into her and strained and strained, she knew he was reaching his release as well.

Moments went by, and she was vaguely aware of her heart rate slowing. Her ragged breaths easing back toward the normal range.

A sense of despair shivered along the nerve endings that had once carried ecstasy.

It was over. And this was probably the last time she would ever be with him.

She let go of the railing, and her fingers trailed along the arm that was still around her, needing a connection that didn't have anything to do with the sex they'd just had.

His fingers caught and gripped hers as he

eased from inside her. He held her there for another minute or two. Then he smiled and scooped her back into his arms. The sense of loss was brief as he kissed her forehead. His words were still spoken in hushed tones. "Do you want to eat? Or visit that bedroom that was mentioned earlier?"

Relief washed across her. Maybe it wasn't over after all.

"Can we eat *after* the bedroom?"

Standing there whispering back and forth was somehow as intimate as what they'd just shared, maybe more.

"Yes, I think that would be my preferred order as well."

With that, he carried her back into the hotel room, closing the balcony door firmly behind him. At least now they were no longer committed to silence. They could both be as loud…and as free…as they wanted.

Diego was gone when she woke up. And he hadn't answered the question she'd asked as they lay in bed together after making love. What the tattoo on his bicep meant. Instead, he'd distracted her with kisses that led to more.

She wasn't surprised to find he'd disappeared. She'd half expected it. In fact, she was glad she wasn't going to have to go through the morning rituals of trying to find small talk that meant nothing and trying to avoid subjects that meant everything.

It had been a night to remember. And she, for one, would remember it all. Every touch. Every whispered word.

Every climax.

She shuddered before showering and getting dressed for her day at the hospital. She and Diego didn't have a joint surgery today, but he had mentioned going to see how Lydia was doing. So she checked her phone for messages—there were none—before driving herself to the hospital and found a spot. Then she hurried into the main entrance of the hospital.

"Well done, Doctor."

The words from Geraldo at the information desk stopped her midflight. She froze. "I'm sorry?"

"What you did yesterday. Everyone's talking about it." The man gave her a huge, goofy grin.

Oh God! How? How could he know? And not just him! Everyone?

Maybe they hadn't been as quiet as they'd thought.

"I—I'm not sure what you're talking about."

Geraldo pulled out his phone and scrolled for a second before turning the screen to face her.

Doctors from Ospedale Maria di Concepción Save Snakebite Victim

Right underneath the caption was a picture of her...and Diego. Not a respectable picture of them at Lydia's side, trying to save her life, but one with her clinging to Diego's back like some kind of sex-starved leech as he'd carried her down the mountain.

Oh, no!

"Where did you find this?" Maybe it was some obscure site. Except he'd said everyone was talking about it.

"It was the first thing that popped up on my browser this morning. I didn't realize the victim was here at the hospital."

"Was?" She and Diego were supposed to visit her this morning.

"She was released a few minutes ago. They said she gave a nice interview."

Oh God. Lydia had talked to the press about what happened? Bree pressed her lids together. Well, the snakebite victim certainly hadn't taken that picture of them, though. She'd been long gone by the time they'd left the scene.

She thought about that couple they'd come across on the path. She thought she remembered the man looking at his phone. But maybe he'd been taking a picture of them instead. *Jeez, Louise*—the expression her mom liked to use popped into her head. It probably didn't look good that the chief of surgery was giving piggyback rides like some sort of sappy boyfriend.

What about a not-so-sappy lover? God, this was a mess. And someone was probably going to guess if they didn't cool things down.

"I—I lost my shoe and couldn't walk."

Geraldo turned the phone around and refreshed the screen. "Ah, I didn't notice you were missing a shoe when I saw it the first time. I thought maybe you guys were celebrating saving that woman."

No, the celebrating had come later.

The thought made her face heat. "It's a long story." She started to say goodbye and walk away, but instead she said, "Thank you for letting me know."

Better to hear about it right as she walked into the hospital than to have no idea their day at Etna had made the papers. Was Diego at work yet? If not, maybe she should warn him before he walked by Geraldo. She moved a short distance away and dialed his number.

He answered on the first ring. "Pintor here."

"Diego, where are you?" Her words came out as a whisper.

"Bree? Why are you talking like that? I'm in my office."

Maybe somehow he'd gotten through without anyone stopping him. Except his words were clipped and blunt—no hint of a greeting there. Or an apology for leaving before she woke up. She raised her voice to a more normal volume. "Have you heard, um…?"

"Heard the news? Yes. Hard to get through that entryway without Geraldo divvying out the latest gossip. This time the gossip just happened to be about us."

Except this wasn't gossip. It had really happened. And if people got the wrong idea about them, they wouldn't be entirely mistaken. There had been more to it than that picture had shown. Much more. Except the sex part wasn't permanent. But a baby certainly was.

"Hey," he said. "Can I call you back? I have someone in my office at the moment."

Had he gotten in trouble for that picture? It wasn't his fault.

"Is it about what happened? Do you need me to come up and explain?"

"No. I don't think that would help in this case."

She shut her eyes, imagining HR sitting in Diego's office demanding an explanation of their conduct. Well, good thing the powers that be hadn't seen the conduct that had happened later that evening. They'd probably both be out on the street, pink slips in hand.

Surely not. What doctors did outside office hours was none of anyone's business, right? Not really. If the heads of Concepción decided she and Diego reflected badly on them, they were allowed to take action. That had been a clause in the hiring document she'd signed. A sense of humiliation engulfed her before she brushed it off angrily. She didn't have anything to be embarrassed about. There was nothing in her paperwork that forbade relationships between coworkers.

A voice that wasn't Diego's came through the phone. "Is that her?" It was a woman, and the tones were clearly peeved. Accusatory. It sounded personal in nature rather than professional.

Was that his ex? His mom?

She heard murmurings that she couldn't make out. Diego must have put his hand over the phone to muffle whatever he was saying. Then he came back. "Let me call you back in a few."

Then the line went dead. Whatever was going on up there wasn't fun. If his ex was upset about a picture, imagine what the woman's surprise would be when she found out Diego had fathered a child with the woman from the picture. *If* the baby was his. Hopefully by Friday they would have their answer.

She waffled from one side to the other as far as who she hoped the father was. It would be a whole lot less complicated if Sergio turned out to be the father. Yes, his parents would want to be in the baby's life, and that would be heartbreaking for her and for them. Especially if the accusations surrounding Sergio turned out to be true.

And if the baby was Diego's?

She'd never even met his parents. Or even knew if they were still alive.

In reality, they didn't know much about each other. Except she knew that Diego was a dedicated doctor and a thorough lover, taking as much care for her pleasure as he had for his own. She'd tried to add to what he was doing, but at times she'd felt like she was floating in a pool of sensuality, so overcome that all she could do was lie there and absorb what was happening.

No wonder he'd taken off. She swallowed. Maybe she owed him an apology.

Five minutes later her phone went off. It was Diego.

"Hi," she said.

"Sorry if you heard any of that."

She tried a guess. "Your ex."

"Yes. She was a little…surprised that I seemed to have moved on so quickly. Not that she doesn't already have a new person in her life."

"Oh." What else could she say? "I hope you got everything worked out."

"There's nothing to work out. We never could agree on a certain point. She asked for permanence, and I didn't want that."

Her belly squelched as she realized she might have given him exactly what he didn't want. And unlike his ex, Bree hadn't asked. But she hadn't tried to corner him into giving something he didn't want. She'd made it more than clear that she didn't expect him to be a permanent fixture in her or the baby's lives.

"I'm sorry, Diego."

She heard him expel a breath. "Don't be. My issues with her have nothing to do with you. Well, maybe they do. Anyway, do you have time to meet for a few minutes so we can decide how to handle all of this new attention?"

"Sure. Do you want to come down here? Or do you want me to go there?"

"Let's meet outside the hospital, if that's

okay. I don't really want anyone to see me disappearing into your office right now."

Ah, she got it. No more secret rendez-vouses for Diego. She should probably be just as concerned, but she wasn't. Eventually her pregnancy was going to make itself known, and everyone was going to be wondering the same thing—whether or not Diego was the father.

What a mess. What she'd thought could be hidden was going to be yanked from behind the curtain and put on full display. All she could do was say the father was no longer in the picture and hope for the best. So much easier to do if Sergio was the father.

"There's a little patio with some tables outside, although people will probably see us. Unlike…"

Last night?

She wasn't going to say it, although there'd been no way to keep it from running through her mind.

He went on. "I'd rather people see us talking and being friendly rather than avoiding each other. That will just make things look worse."

She agreed with him, although, boy, did

avoiding him ever sound attractive right now. "Okay, the patio it is. Five minutes?"

"Yes. I'll meet you down there."

Bree ducked into the coffee shop on her way to her destination, being stopped a couple more times by colleagues congratulating her on her quick thinking.

Damn, it wasn't like she'd grabbed the snake by the throat or anything. Even the thought of that made her shudder. She glanced down at her feet, glad she hadn't worn her new thong sandals. She wasn't sure she would wear those anywhere around Diego again. Because when he'd finally removed her shoes last night, he had massaged her feet and toes, giving her an entirely different kind of pleasure. It had been tender and romantic and nothing like she'd experienced before. But the sweet and the sexy had all kind of merged into one blissful night. Even looking at those sandals made those memories come into sharp relief.

Her coffee in hand, she pushed through the door to the outside patio area. A huge pergola covered the space; its canvas covering could be pulled to give shade to those out there or retracted to bring warmth in the winter. Diego was already out there, hunched over one of the tables. There were only a couple of other people on the patio, and they were seated quite some distance away. Glancing at the coffee in her hand, she wished she'd asked him if he wanted anything. Moving over to him, she picked the seat across the table from him. "Sorry that this thing kind of blew up in our faces."

"Yeah. Me, too. I was focused on the talk we were going to have yesterday, and it never dawned on me that anyone would find out and misconstrue things so completely."

"Misconstrue them how?"

"That we're in a relationship."

It was exactly what she'd feared when Geraldo had waylaid her this morning. And even though she knew in her heart of hearts they weren't emotionally involved with each other, the words still stung with a sense of rejection. "All we can do is tell them, if they ask. Just say that I asked you about Mount Etna and that you felt obligated to take me on a tour. The rest is history."

"So lie, in other words?"

She shrugged. "What do you suggest we do, then?"

"I have no idea."

"Does this have to do with your ex coming to see you? Does she see that article as somehow confirming something?"

"No. She doesn't. I think she was just feeling me out to see if I'd changed my mind."

"About what?"

He gave a hard laugh. "About having children. That me saying it wasn't her, it was me had been something I'd made up so I could go out and make a child with someone else."

"You broke up with her because you didn't want kids?" Her heart seized. "Did I miss you telling me this? I thought you said it was about permanence."

"Is there anything more permanent than having a child together?" He squeezed the bridge of his nose between his thumb and forefinger. "Anyway, I didn't think it was relevant. But it wasn't the only reason Selina and I called it quits."

But it was the main one, or the woman wouldn't have come looking for him. "She has another boyfriend?"

"Yes, and she didn't hide the fact that they're trying to get pregnant."

God, Bree and Diego hadn't even *tried* to have kids. It had been the furthest thing from either of their minds, and yet here they were.

"Did you tell her? About my condition?"

"No. I didn't see the need."

Because it might not be his. Or maybe because he wasn't planning on sticking around. The sting from earlier came back stronger than ever.

"So what did you tell her about that picture? And what do you want me to say when people stop and ask me?"

"Just tell them the truth. That we were hiking up Etna and came across someone who needed help."

He was right. Said like that, it seemed about as innocent as you could get.

"Well, that's what I told Geraldo. And I told him I'd lost a shoe and that's what the picture was showing. He hadn't even noticed, he said. Hopefully that will help head off a lot of gossip."

"You and me both."

She decided to say something that she

hoped would help him feel less pressure. "I don't expect you to make any kind of decision until after we find out the results of the test, which is just two days away—if they're on time with it."

"I have thought about it, and what I'd like to propose is this. That if this baby has my DNA, we use the pregnancy as a testing ground for you to see how I do. To see how I handle the pressures involved with being a father. And then sometime before the baby is born, you can make the final decision about what role I play."

If this baby has my DNA... That phrasing was about as impersonal as you could get. It rubbed her wrong and kept rubbing until a raw spot opened up in her heart.

So he was going to act like the baby's father during the pregnancy, but he was going to be passive about it? Was going to make *her* choose whether or not he was involved? What about him? What did Diego want?

And if it wasn't the rosy experience he wanted it to be? She wasn't sure why, but that suggestion just made the DNA comment even worse. He'd said the wrong thing…on the wrong day. And she wasn't having it.

"I'm sorry, Diego. But that is absolutely not an option. You're either in this baby's life or you're not."

CHAPTER NINE

DIEGO WASN'T SURE what he'd been expecting her to say, but that wasn't it. She'd cut him off without even giving him a chance.

"Don't you think it's better to do the test run now before the baby is born than after he or she has come into the world?"

She frowned and took a big drink of the coffee she'd brought. "I don't understand you. You were just worried about people thinking we were in a relationship, so you going with me to prenatal visits isn't going to look the least bit suspicious?"

He leaned back in his chair. "I wasn't exactly going to advertise that we were going together."

"I don't think we exactly advertised our trip up to Etna, either, and look what happened with that."

"What do you expect me to do, Bree? Suddenly confess to being the baby's father after he or she is born?"

"No." Her voice was low and firm. "I don't expect you to do anything. And I really don't want to make any kind of decision until after we get the results back from the paternity test."

"And then what? We were supposed to make plans when we were at Etna, so why the sudden about-face?" He'd just had a completely exasperating meeting with Selina, and now to have to sit here and hash out things about the baby he thought he'd never have? It wasn't sitting well.

"I don't know. Maybe we weren't supposed to talk on Etna. The bottom line is I don't want to make plans for what I don't know. Not yet. And I certainly don't want to make plans for you."

Two women came out onto the terrace area, trays with food in their hands. They sat down at the next table, looked at them and then leaned across to say something to each other. Great. So much for talking this out. It looked like everyone else was talking about Bree and him…except for Bree and him.

She tipped the cup up, taking what must be the last swig of coffee and swallowing it. "Why don't we hold off on this until I go on Friday?"

This was the first he'd heard of this: that she was going in person to get their test results. Well, if she could be there, then so could he.

So, very aware that there were people at the next table, he murmured. "Great. So what time should I pick you up?"

Her eyes widened as she, too, glanced at the next table. "You don't have to do that."

"That's where you're wrong, Bree. I want to. And then we can decide things right then and right there." He stood up and gave her a smile that felt grotesquely fake. But he wasn't going to give her a chance to argue about it any more than she'd given him a chance to argue his point about trying fatherhood on for size. "I'll see you then."

Bree had been a little hasty in shooting down Diego's idea. And once she had a chance to think about it, she saw that it had merit. Hadn't she been afraid he would suddenly disappear from the baby's life like Sergio had disappeared from hers? And how could she ask him to decide on something he couldn't try on for size? Something he'd have no idea how he'd feel about until he experienced it. She'd been able to make a choice about having the baby. Wasn't it only fair that she allow him to make the best choice he could under the circumstances?

But she also didn't want to take another two-hour trek over to Palermo trapped in a car with him. So she'd called Teresina, the friend she had made over at the other hospital, and asked if she could have the results delivered to her house. Because if they drove over there together, her mind was going to drift off into areas she shouldn't revisit. That she couldn't revisit. The last two days had been torture as far as her work at the hospital went. She had been approached by person after person and given congratulatory words, when any one of them would have done the same thing under the circumstances. Worse, the hospital had blown up a copy of the story and put it on one of the bulletin boards, where patients could see it.

Including the picture of Diego packing her around on his back.

But fortunately, HR had never called her in to ask her about that day. For that she was very glad. If Diego was to be a father to this child, then that would have to change. They would have to go together to talk to the people who handled personnel matters and inform them. And what then? Would they ask her to resign? Things could get ugly if she and Diego ever disagreed over things like custody or visitation. Because although they weren't romantically involved, they would have to come to a consensus on how they would make decisions. Would the baby have her last name? Or Diego's? A million choices that never would have had to be made if he hadn't seen the pregnancy test in her basket that day.

Would she have told him if he hadn't been there that day? She wasn't sure. Although, she was almost certain he would have asked at some point because of the timing, and because he'd known next to nothing about her relationship with Sergio. Of course, now he knew a lot more than he'd bargained for.

Bree was supposed to call him once the

results were couriered to her hotel, and they would meet and discuss them. Was she going to look at them ahead of time? Probably not. The last thing she wanted was to be tempted to back out of meeting him. And if she found out the baby was Diego's, she might. So her plan was to open them together.

Probably another mistake. But honestly, she didn't want to be alone when she found out.

But she didn't want to be with Diego, either.

So it was a no-win situation. But she would get through it the same way she'd gotten through the day of her wedding, the way she'd gotten through the results of that pregnancy test. They way she'd gotten through the news of their trip to Etna being broadcast far and wide. She'd weathered all those things. She would weather this, too.

The hotel's reception desk called and said she had a package down at the lobby. Her heart skipped a beat. This was it. The moment of truth.

She went downstairs and picked up the official-looking envelope, glad that the paper was thick enough to keep prying eyes from seeing what was inside. Including hers.

Then rather than go back upstairs, where the temptation to tear it open and look would be too much, she went and sat in one of the chairs in the lobby. They hadn't talked about where they would meet to find out the results. But she didn't want to be upstairs in her room. And she didn't want to go to Diego's house.

In fact, the sooner she could move her things out of this hotel, the better. The memories here were just...overwhelming. Every time she went out onto that balcony, she felt him all around her. And damn if it didn't hurt. In a way that it shouldn't hurt. Unless she cared about him more than she wanted to admit.

Pulling her phone from her purse, she dialed his number. He picked up on the first ring. "Did you get it?"

"I did. Where do you want to meet?"

They sounded like two spies planning some kind of covert op. And maybe they were, kind of. They were trying to keep something from people at the hospital, although after that fiasco with Etna, she wasn't sure it was even possible. But at least they could keep this part between just the two of them.

"How about at the lower parking area of Etna? We can talk in the car. In private."

Yes, that would work. In fact, she couldn't imagine a better place to do that. "Okay, do you want to meet there?"

"Why don't I just pick you up and we'll go from there. Fifteen minutes?"

"Sounds good. I'm already in the lobby, so just pull up in front of the hotel. I'll be watching for you." With that they hung up, and Bree prayed they could work this out. Because the sooner they could do that, the sooner they could put all this behind them. At least, she hoped they could.

She was outside when Diego pulled up. She slid into the passenger seat and hoped he couldn't see the worry swirling around inside her. Well, judging from his tight jaw and the muscle working in there, she wasn't the only one. Whatever was in that envelope wouldn't change things for her as much as it would for him. Unless he decided to walk.

Only she was going to wave a white flag

and suggest they do what he'd wanted to do and give things a trial run, but more for his sake than hers. He needed to be sure about this more than she did.

So that meant they would need to travel to Palermo together for her prenatal appointments. Which she assumed was part of what he'd meant when he talked about that.

He glanced at her. "Do you know?"

She knew what he meant. "No. I…" Suddenly it was hard for her to see. "I didn't want to open it on my own."

A hand touched her, fingers lacing through the one in her lap. "I understand. We'll get through this together."

"I haven't even told my parents. I wasn't sure how to. I thought I'd wait until after I had the results, but if the baby's not Sergio's…" She swallowed a ball of regret. "I'm not quite sure how to explain it."

"Maybe you won't need to."

She shut her eyes. She had made such a mess about everything. Maybe she should have terminated, even gone to another country if necessary to have it done. But even the thought of that made her belly ache deep inside. She'd longed for a baby, and Sergio had felt an equal desire to have kids. Despite everything, this seemed like the right thing to do. For her. Whether or not it was the right thing for Diego was another subject entirely.

I would find a way.

His words on Mount Etna came back to her. Except he'd broken up with someone he cared about because she wanted kids and he didn't. It had been a deal breaker for him. And Bree wanted more than one. Whether that would ever happen or not…

But she would need to be honest with Diego about that as well. Because that might cause even more complications for him. How did you take one child—your child—on outings and leave the other behind? As a mom, how could she allow that? And if she found someone who would love them all equally and married him? So many hard, hard things to wade through.

"Maybe you're right and I won't have to." But in the pit of her stomach was a growing fear that this child might very well *not* belong to her late fiancé. And might belong to a man she'd spent a single night with.

Well, make that two nights. And actually,

the baby was the whole reason they'd spent that second night together.

They got to the parking area and Diego found a space at the far back corner, since they weren't going to get out and hike this time. He left the car running and shifted in his seat to look at her. He'd unlinked their hands to shift gears a few minutes ago, but he reached over again and gave hers a squeeze. "I want you to know that even if this baby isn't mine, I will support you in any way I have time to."

In any way he had time to? That was an odd way to phrase things, but she nodded and said thank you. She had a feeling he'd be a lot more empathetic to her situation if the baby was Sergio's and not his. What did that say about his chances of seeing this thing through to the end? It was one thing to explain why "Uncle" Diego didn't come around to visit anymore, but to explain why Daddy didn't care—or couldn't care? They were both equally damning.

"Well, I guess I should open it." She pulled free and held the envelope.

But when her hands were shaking too much to get her thumb under the flap, he took it from her and set it on his lap, then, cupping her chin, he looked at her. "It's going to be okay, Bree. I promise."

How could he promise that when he couldn't even guarantee he was going to be there for the baby? But she would be there. And she had love enough for two people. So she nodded at him. "I know it is."

And for the first time, she thought maybe it was.

Diego had no idea why he'd said that. But watching Bree struggle with her emotions, listening to her talk about her fear about telling her parents and then seeing those hands so skilled in perfusion shake at the thought of this baby's fate had gotten to him. But she was stronger than she knew. And she was good at everything she did. He had no doubt she would be equally good at being a mom. His own mother had raised two boys practically on her own with minimal help from his father. If his mom could do it, Bree could, too.

And what about you?

A question he couldn't answer. Not yet.

"Ready?" he asked her.

She nodded.

Diego ripped open the envelope and pulled out the sheet inside. On it were a bunch of numbers in two columns. He held it down so Bree could see it, too, as he tried to make it out. Then he realized one of them was for Bree and the other was for him. At the bottom of the test were the words *The alleged father is not excluded as the biological father of the fetus.* The percentages were listed as ninety-nine point…followed by a bunch of other nines.

Well, now he knew. Now they both knew.

He was this baby's father.

A big part of him had hoped he wasn't. No decisions. No responsibilities. No angst.

Instead, he was faced with all three.

But there was something else there. Some weird thread of emotion that he'd never experienced before. But he was absolutely not going to set Bree up for disappointment by impulsively jumping in with both feet. He was going to do what he did before any surgery. Deliberate. Think about what could go wrong. About what could go right. Plan out each step and have an exit strategy in mind if one part didn't go as planned.

Exit? This wasn't surgery, where he could just abort the procedure if things started going wrong. This was a baby's life. It's happiness.

Still, it was the only strategy he knew. He could approach And if it turned out this was inoperable because of who he was as a person?

Well, then, yes, he was going to have his exit strategy planned out far in advance, when it would do the least amount of damage to Bree or the baby.

"Well, it looks like Sergio didn't get the winning ticket this time."

She gave him a look that bordered on a glare. "You didn't think of it as much of a winning ticket, either, from what I remember."

"I phrased that badly. I'm sorry."

Closing her eyes for a second before looking at him, she squinched her nose up. "I'm the one who's sorry. None of this is your fault."

"It's not yours, either."

"So it's neither of our fault, and yet here we are." She stared at the paper for a minute before taking it from him and stuffing it back in the envelope. "Thoughts? Or do you need time to process?"

"Yes. To both questions."

"Okay, let's hear the thoughts part."

"I know you said you didn't want to take me on a test run as a father and see how I do—and for *me* to see how I do, but—"

She held up a hand. "Right after I said that, I realized I was wrong to shoot you down like I did." She licked her lips. "So how would this 'test run' play out, exactly?"

"I would go to your appointments with you. See how my schedule can be rearranged." He decided to be honest with her. "My dad was not there for my brother and me. Ever. My parents were married, but my mom raised us single-handedly. Oh, he handed her a check every week and took care of us financially, but he was barely home. Maybe three or four hours a week."

"A week? And your mom put up with that?"

"I think she was scared to leave him and not have a safety net, since her parents were both gone already. But once we were out of the house, they divorced. My father remarried less than a year later. And he had another set of kids, twins this time. We never knew them. Because my dad wasn't there for them, either. This time, though, his wife didn't wait around for them to grow up. She left him and moved to a different part of Italy, and none of us heard from her again."

"Why did he even have kids, if he didn't want them?"

His eyes came up and met hers. "That is the question, isn't it? I think he thought getting married and having kids was an expected part of life. But it's a mistake I don't want to make. I am invested in my job probably just as much as my father ever was. I see it. I know it. And yet it's hard for me to let go. I do not want my kids to have the kind of father I would be at this point in my life. Which is why I wanted to see if I could change my priorities."

"Where is your father now?"

"He's dead."

Bree went pale. "He died?"

"Three years ago. Of a heart attack."

"And that's not reason enough for you to make a change?"

He sighed. "I have made some. The question is, can I make enough of them to do some good for someone other than my patients?"

"I see. So this trial period is to see if a leopard can change its spots."

"That's it in a nutshell."

She nodded. "Well, this is your chance to try. Only I promise you, if I think you aren't going to be able to hack it, you won't need to step in and fire yourself. I'll be there to personally hand you that dismissal form." She smiled, as if to take some of the sting out of it. And it did. It also gave him some reassurance that she didn't need him for a paycheck like his mom had done with his dad. This woman was strong enough to push him away if she thought it was best for her and her child. And she'd already told him she didn't want his money.

So he was going to take her at her word and let her stand back and observe how real his commitment turned out to be. Surely with both of them wanting what was best for this baby, they would come to a decision. The right one. For everyone involved.

"I'll hold you to that dismissal form. I don't want you to cut me any slack. Because I'm not going to cut myself any, either. Okay?"

"You've got yourself a deal, Probationary Partner. Now let's see if we can get this kid and his or her mother something to eat. Because she is starving."

"One dinner coming up. How about if I take you to a swanky little place I know that's not too far from here?"

"As long as they have food that won't poison us, I'll take almost anything."

CHAPTER TEN

BREE'S PHONE RANG. Peeling her eyelids apart, she rolled to the side and struggled to focus the clock. It took three tries before the lighted numbers made any sense.

Two a.m.

She came fully awake. No one called in the middle of the night unless something was very wrong. Her parents? She spun her phone toward her. If this was a crank call...

Diego's name showed in big white letters.

It had been almost a week since they'd had their talk at the base of Mount Etna and, so far, life had carried on as normal. She saw him in passing, and they smiled at each other. And the ruckus at the hospital over piggyback-gate was slowly winding down. Like her eyelids, which were drifting back together. The phone buzzed again.

Wake up, Bree!

Panic started swirling through her, memories of talking to a police officer after Sergio's accident.

The confusion. The fear. The numbness afterward.

She snatched the phone up and pressed the answer button even as she was sitting up. "Hello?"

Her voice was high-pitched and unsteady. She tried to punch back the sensation of fear.

"Bree, we need you down at the hospital if there's any way you can get here."

"Diego…" She went slack with relief when she realized it was his voice, not some stranger's. "It's you."

"Yes, of course it's me." There was a curt impatience in his tone that she didn't understand. "Can you come?"

"You need a perfusionist at this time of night?" Normally heart surgeries were scheduled during daytime or afternoon hours. If they needed her now… Her fingers tightened on the phone.

"We have a patient with infective endocarditis in her mitral valve. Severe regurge. She's not going to make it without immediate surgery." There was a pause. A long one, where she thought she'd lost the signal. Then his voice came back. "She's also twenty-one weeks pregnant."

Her stomach lurched, and her free hand went to her lower belly and pressed. Twenty-one weeks. The baby wasn't old enough to deliver before surgery. Her mind ran through the case studies she'd read of pregnant women who'd been put on cardiopulmonary bypass for surgery or other reasons. There was a narrow margin of error, and sometimes the baby didn't make it. The mortality rate could be as high as eighteen percent.

If Diego was calling her, it meant that he was the only one who could tackle this and be successful, since he was the best heart surgeon on the island. He was this woman's best chance for survival. Her baby's best chance.

"I'll be there in fifteen minutes." Tossing the phone onto the table, she leaped out of bed and grabbed a set of scrubs from one of her drawers and yanked everything into place. Taking time only to drag a brush through her hair and to brush her teeth, she was out the door in five minutes, rushing down the stairs rather than waiting on the elevator.

She fired up her car and headed north. She'd never seen so little traffic on the streets of Catania, and she made it to Concepción two minutes earlier than she'd predicted. Jamming the gearshift into Park, she got out and sprinted up to the hospital entrance, her mind going through everything she needed to do and the precautions they needed to take.

Diego was nowhere to be seen when she burst through the doors, but she was sure he was either with the patient or already scrubbing in. Fortunately she kept the bypass machine at the ready, checking on it every single time she arrived or left the hospital.

After she took the elevator to the third floor, where the surgical ward was, a nurse met her at the doors. "He said go ahead and get set up. They'll start as soon as you're ready."

"Everyone else is already here?"

"Yes."

How could that be?

Nerves kicked in. She normally had more time to prepare, but these kinds of cases didn't always follow a set schedule. And today, time was of the essence. If the mother didn't survive, then the baby had no chance at all.

She got ready and then gloved up and entered the room. Diego was already there, as was the patient and the entire surgical team. All except her. The nurse was right.

How had they all gotten here so fast? Had she been the last person to be called?

Maybe Diego hadn't thought they'd need to put her on bypass. But with endocarditis and a destroyed mitral valve? That was unlikely.

Getting in her station, she checked that they'd gotten everything she needed. Diego must have arranged to have this set up already, too. He came over. "Are you okay to do this?"

"What do you mean by okay?"

He frowned above his mask and said in a low voice, "I mean because of the patient."

She still had no clue what he was talking about. Wait, did she know this person?

No, she didn't see how she could.

Oh! Realization dawned. Because the patient was pregnant! Was that why she felt so late to the game and why everyone else was already here? Had he scrambled around trying to find any other perfusionist before calling her?

Her nerves unwound, and a thin thread of anger took its place. Yes, Bree was pregnant. But Diego was going to be a father, too. Did he feel he was somehow immune from feeling fear for their patient and her baby? Bree was certainly able to put herself in the patient's shoes and, hell yes, it scared her to death to think of something like this happening to her and her baby. Diego should feel that, too. Shouldn't he?

She sat up straight and looked him in the eye. "I'm fine. Just tell me what the plan is."

The surgeon filled her in, letting her know the specific changes they would make for this particular surgery. The goal was to not only save the mother, but to maintain the pregnancy as well.

"You have the replacement valve here already?"

"Yes. Porcine this time."

"Okay. Anything I should know about her blood work?" She needed to focus on the patient and not on what Diego had or hadn't done.

"Because of the severity of the regurgitation, there's some evidence of hypoxia."

"And the baby?"

"So far, the fetus is hanging in there."

Hanging in there. But not thriving. "Let me check a few more things. Is there a neonatologist here, just in case?"

Diego looked at her, and she could have sworn she saw something flicker behind his eyes. The first indication of true empathy, although if so, he'd hidden it admirably. "Yes, he's standing right over there by the fetal monitor, but at twenty-one weeks…"

"I know. So let's do all we can to have a good outcome."

His expression returned to the stoic neutral man she was coming to know. "That's all I ever want. A good outcome."

The words gave her pause. Yes, he'd been repeating her statement, but there was an inflection there that made her wonder if it was just about the surgery at hand. But right now she couldn't worry about that. Or about anything other than doing her job.

Less than a half hour later, Diego was

making his first incision. It was hard not to let her gaze keep drifting to the fetal monitor, which was keeping track of variations in the baby's heart rate. The real test would be when the patient went on bypass. Surgeries like this one were not done every day, and the thinking was to hold off, whenever possible, until late in the third trimester, when the baby could be delivered by caesarean before valve-replacement surgery was performed. That was the best option. But the best option wasn't always available. Sometimes you had to salvage what you could from a bad situation.

She shifted on her stool as inferences from that statement coiled around her brain's amygdala, squeezing emotions from it that she didn't want or need right now.

Forcing her attention back to her job and away from Diego and her pregnancy, she settled in for the long haul. She could hash this out with her heart and her brain later. And she needed to leave the patient in the hands of those who knew what they were doing. The ones who would pay attention to the baby's stats and the mom's. She just needed to do her very best to give the team what they needed.

So far, things were progressing the way they should. Diego was in the chest cavity, getting the vessels hooked up for bypass. Her part was coming soon. And she was right where she needed to be. Where she wanted to be. In this room.

She tried not to think about his possible reasons for trying to lock her out of this case, if he'd even done that. She wouldn't know unless she asked. And that would have to wait.

Sergio had wanted her to be a stay-at-home mom, but when she'd stood up for herself, he'd given in, maybe realizing he would be dooming their relationship if he tried to push the matter.

And Diego. What did he think? After all, Bree was replacing a woman who'd made that very decision: to stay home with her baby. There was no right or wrong path here, each individual had to do what was right for them and their family, but Bree knew she needed to be in the operating room. It was part of her DNA.

"Ready for bypass."

Diego's voice brought her back to the task at hand. Twisting some knobs and checking levels, she glanced up at him and nodded. "Commencing bypass."

Blood flowed through the lines and through the machine, which would oxygenate it and push it through a heat exchanger as it prepared to pump it back into the patient.

There were a tense few minutes while everyone waited to see how the baby would handle the CPB. So far, the heart rate hadn't fluctuated, but that could always change if the baby didn't get exactly what it needed from the machine. It was up to Bree to make sure that baby got every molecule of oxygen it required.

She kept her eyes on her panel readings, watching for problems, signs that something was going wrong.

So far, everything was steady. Which worried her. It was going a little too well.

"I'm ready for the valve."

It was amazing how quiet it was in here today. It was as if everyone knew what was at stake. A lot of times there were jokes or light camaraderie to relieve tension, and some surgeons liked to have music on. For some, the louder the better. But this particular room was bathed in concentration. It was palpable.

She glanced up to see the pig valve being handed over to Diego. She watched him examine it for defects, those long fingers turning it this way and then that. Then her attention was right back on her instruments.

The neonatologist's voice broke through the silence.

"There was a blip. And now a slight drop in heart rate. A little more."

He was talking about the baby's heart rate, not the mom's. She hurriedly checked the fluid reservoir, knowing if it dropped too low, air could enter the chamber, causing a fatal embolism. But it was fine. Nothing had changed on her table. Oxygen saturation levels were steady.

Diego stopped what he was doing and waited.

Finally the other doctor said, "We're coming back up. Not sure what that was, but we need to keep this moving."

"I need another half hour to forty-five minutes. Okay to continue?"

The neonatologist nodded. "You have to.

I don't see any exit strategy that carries a positive outcome for either of them."

Out of the corner of her eye, she saw Diego's head whip up to stare at the man. That was strange. She'd never seen him do that before.

His jaw was tight for a second or two before he responded. "Neither do I. We have to do what's best for both of them. And that's to remove the damaged part and take it out of the picture."

There was an air of resignation about the way he said that that made a bubble of uneasiness rise up in her stomach before popping. Another took its place, and then another and another. Just like the air embolism she'd been worried about.

He got back to work, giving his commentaries as he went through each step. Part of that was so that everything was on the official record, but in Bree's experience, they were also crossing things off their grocery list of items that had to be completed during surgery.

"Valve is in place. Checking suture line." He paused. "How's the fetus?"

"Holding steady."

Diego glanced at Bree and then looked away. "Ready to restore blood flow to the heart."

A few more tense seconds went by, and then the patient's heart monitor started registering activity. "I've got a heartbeat."

"Baby is hanging in there." The neonatologist sounded relieved.

It was funny how different people referred to an unborn child. Because she was pregnant, she tended to think of her own baby as a...well, baby.

It doesn't mean anything that Diego is using the word fetus. *It's the correct technical term. Right? The one most medical professionals use.*

But there had been something about the way he'd looked at the neonatologist earlier when he'd talked about exit strategies... About how he said they needed to do what was best for them, meaning mother and baby.

"Let's wean her off bypass."

Her. The mother. As if that was the only individual who mattered.

Could a leopard really change it spots?

Her words to Diego came back to her.

She shook off the growing number of worries that now seemed to be lobbed at her one after the other as she did her best to deflect them. Maybe Diego had been right to try to find someone else.

No. If anyone would work hard for this patient and that precious cargo she was carrying, it was Bree. And she had every right to be in this room.

"Weaning off now." She turned the knobs, slowly transitioning her machine's duties back onto to the patient. The baby's heart rate spiked for a couple of seconds, and she closed her eyes, breathing a silent prayer. Hopefully it was due to the normal change in blood pressure after coming off bypass. Then the heart rate slid back to normal once again.

"Oxygen sats are holding steady. Normal sinus rhythm. No leakage." Diego glanced around the room but skipped over her. Just like he had during their very first surgery together. She swallowed hard. Had she wanted him to give her that secretive smile she loved so much? A slight nod to let her know everything was okay?

Yes. But there'd been nothing.

God. So much had happened since that first surgery. So very much.

But had anything really changed?

She didn't know. But right now it felt like her stomach was being squeezed in a vise that kept tightening with every beat of her heart.

"And baby is doing fine, thank God."

The words of the neonatologist echoed in her skull. Yes, thank God. This time Bree let her own forearm press on her lower belly. Her baby was fine, too. And he or she would be fine. With or without Diego.

But holy hell, she wanted him there. And that seemed to be the biggest tragedy of all.

"Okay, let's close her up. We'll need her on IV antibiotics for a few days and by mouth after that to make sure the other valves stay safe."

Diego's low, reassuring voice continued as they worked to close things in stages, ending with the skin.

Only it didn't reassure her. Not like it once had.

And when the surgeon was finished and all his checks had been completed, he left the room. Before she'd finished cleaning up her station. Only this time, she wasn't stalling. And this time, she knew Diego wouldn't be standing right outside the room waiting on her. He had fled the scene. Just like Sergio had on their wedding day. And she had no idea why.

Diego sat in his office, staring at the computer image of a patient's file. Lorenzo Portini's words during his surgery had sent an electric shock through him. He knew it was common for doctors to talk about exit strategies, but to hear it so soon after he'd mentally gone through his own checklists of being a father had sent him reeling. Was it coincidence? Or was someone trying to tell him something?

Dios! His patient had survived the surgery. So had the fetus. But there were other things that could happen even afterward. Preterm labor. Premature delivery. Oxygen deprivation to the fetus despite their every effort. Those blips on the monitor had meant something. Except no one knew what. Not yet. Maybe not ever.

A knock sounded at his door. "Come in."

Bree slid through the door, and his heart

sank. He should have stayed after the surgery. He'd just needed time to…process. But what he was supposed to be processing, he wasn't sure.

This time Bree didn't wait to be asked to sit. She walked over and sank into one of the chairs, looking at him with steady eyes.

"Can I ask you a question?"

"Sure." He said the word, but the last thing he wanted right now were questions.

"Did you try to find another perfusionist before calling me?"

Dannazione! Had someone told her he'd scrambled for almost a half hour before dialing her number? "What do you mean?"

She leaned forward. "I don't think it's a difficult question, Diego. Did. You. Call. Someone. Else?"

"Yes." He wasn't going to lie to her.

"Why?"

He'd asked himself that same question. "I'm not sure. It was a pregnant mom. I thought it might…" He paused for a long time before saying the words, realizing for the first time how they sounded. "I thought it might upset you."

"You thought it might upset *me*. But it wouldn't upset *you*?"

"Of course it did. Any time someone comes in with heart problems, there's always a chance that—"

"No." Bree rubbed a thumb along the sharp edge of his desk, the way she might check to see how damaging something could be. "I'm not talking about the upset that comes with a generic case. I'm talking about the concern that comes with putting yourself in the other person's shoes. Of wondering the normal what-ifs that come with the thought that it might be *your* baby whose life is on the line. I certainly thought it."

"I had a job to do."

"Yes. Well, so did I. One that you tried to keep me from doing."

He leaned back in his chair and crossed his arms over his chest. "I'm sorry if it seemed that way."

The second he said the words, he realized it wasn't a real apology. He was pushing it back onto her, saying it was all about her perception. But it wasn't. She was right. He had called around, trying to get someone else. And had wasted valuable time in the process.

Before she could call him out on it, he sighed. "No, you're right. I did try to keep you from coming. And I don't know why, other than what I've already told you. That I wasn't sure how hard this case would be on you."

"That's for me to decide, don't you think?"

He decided to move to the heart of the matter. "Look, Bree. When my dad wasn't there for us, my mom always was. She was there. Every single time I or my brother needed her."

"Are you saying I won't be for our child?"

"No, but if I somehow can't…"

Bree went completely still when his voice trailed away. "If you can't what?"

"I want to make sure that someone will be there for this child."

"Which child? *Ours?*" Her lips thinned. "There will be someone there for the baby. I will be. Whether you are or not. But that doesn't mean I'm going to sit at home 24-7. Or avoid cases that might prove to be painful. I want to work. I love my job, and I want my son or daughter to know that it's okay to go after your own dreams. That you can have both. You can love someone *and* be there for them while still pursuing your goals. They're not mutually exclusive. It's all about balance."

"What if you can't? What if *I* can't?"

She shrugged. "I don't know. I guess you're going to have to do some soul-searching and see how you want to spend the next fifty or so years of your life. Is work enough to fulfill you? If it is, then… Well, I'd rather know that now." She closed her eyes. "No, not now. But soon. Think about it. And when you've decided, come and talk to me."

With that she stood and came around to his side of the desk and dropped a kiss on his cheek. One that burned like fire and seared his soul.

"And if you decide you can't, I'll be okay. We both will."

She left his office with a quiet click of the door, leaving him staring at the chair she'd just occupied. And wondering what the hell was wrong with him.

CHAPTER ELEVEN

IT HAD BEEN more than a week since she'd left Diego's office, and she'd heard nothing from the cardiac surgeon. Worse, she'd noticed on the staffing board that he'd performed two surgeries since then. One was another valve replacement and one had been a triple bypass. Bree had been called in for neither of them. She'd been devastated. She thought he cared about her. At least on some level. Evidently she was wrong.

Horribly, over the last week, she'd come to realize she loved the man. Loved everything about him.

But that didn't mean they were destined to be together. She couldn't force him to love her back. Or to want to stay with her. Or even to love their child.

He was an honorable man, so she felt like

he would try like hell to be in the baby's life, but how fair was that of her to expect something he didn't feel he could give?

And if he didn't even feel like he could work with her in surgery— Well, that wasn't a good sign.

She'd had other work, so it wasn't like she was out of a job if Diego never wanted to work with her again. There were a couple of other cardiologists attached to the hospital. And she'd gone to a neighboring hospital in the middle of the night to help with a difficult surgery while their perfusionist was on vacation. The feeling of having a foot in two worlds had shifted over the last week to having a foot in *three* worlds—Sicily being the newest member of that club. And yet she belonged to none of those clubs. Not really.

She'd reached out to her parents last night via video chat and told them about the pregnancy and shared a little bit about what had happened since then. Once she started, she hadn't been able to stop the tears from flowing. Her dad had offered to come and beat up whoever had hurt her. That had finally gotten a laugh out of her.

"I don't need violence," she'd said. "I need advice. What should I do?"

"Come home." Her parents had said the words in unison.

Home. Where there were people who loved her and would help her with the pregnancy and all that came afterward.

So today, Bree was sitting at the small table in her hotel room with the papers for the house she'd planned to buy laid out in front of her. The deadline for putting pen to paper and closing on it was today. If she went through with it, she would be entering a contract that would be difficult to withdraw from. She would already lose her deposit. But if she signed, she stood to lose a lot more.

Yes, she did. And not just monetarily.

She stood to lose emotionally by staying in Catania.

And what if Diego decided he wanted to be in his child's life?

How long did she intend to wait? It had been a week. Did she wait a month? Wait until after the baby was born? Wait until he or she was eighteen?

No. She wasn't going to allow her life or

the life of her child to remain in some kind of limbo. She needed to move forward. With or without Diego.

And from the looks of it, he was going to choose the "without" clause. What had he said during that surgery? Something about doing what was best for the mother and fetus. And that meant taking the damaged part out of the picture.

She'd thought it was a weird way to word it at the time. In fact, he'd seemed agitated, jerking to look at the neonatologist as if coming to a realization. Diego had struggled and struggled hard, from the sound of it, with how little involvement his dad had had in his life. Maybe that's what he'd meant in his office about wanting to make sure her baby had someone he or she could count on. Because he wasn't expecting the child—or Bree—to be able to count on him.

A spear of pain went through her.

Well, at least he'd been honest about it. Painfully honest, unlike Sergio. And what had he gotten for it? Lambasted by her and prodded to hurry up and decide.

Had she been unfair to him? Maybe. But looking back, she thought some of her insistence might have come out of fear. Fear of being alone. Fear of a second person who seemed to be all in and then suddenly exiting her life. Although, what she felt for Diego eclipsed what she'd ever felt for Sergio. It was awful and made her realize she'd had no business getting engaged to him.

So no more prodding Diego or going to him to ask for a commitment. This time, she was going to be the one who let go.

So what did she do about the house? Did she go forward with it and face the next seven months of her pregnancy wondering if she was going to be able to find a birth coach? Going to prenatal appointments by herself? Answer awful, probing questions about whose baby it was?

And seeing Diego as they passed in the hallway, when she was as big as a house? When he was thanking his lucky stars that he'd gotten out while he still could?

God, she couldn't do it.

Come home.

The words whispered through her head like a siren's song. It wasn't true that she didn't belong anywhere. She had a family who loved her, and she was about to form her only little family, consisting of her and the baby. And maybe she would add to that number after a while using a sperm bank.

And suddenly she knew what she was going to do. She picked up the contract and slid it—unsigned—back into the envelope it had been delivered in. Then she got up from the kitchen table with the envelope and her phone in hand and made the call.

It was answered on the second ring. "Romildi Realty."

"Hello, Tania? Do you have a few minutes to meet with me this afternoon? I'm afraid I have some bad news."

Diego exited the nondescript gray building he'd been visiting for the last couple of weeks. There was no sign advertising who resided in there or what they did. In fact, if he hadn't gotten the center's name from a friend, he would have never known about the meetings that went on inside every Monday, Wednesday and Friday. It wasn't that he was ashamed to be seen there. He wasn't. But what he had needed was to understand what was going on inside his head. And why he seemed dead set on embodying the same traits that he'd claimed to hate.

He wasn't the only one in that situation, it seemed. And when he'd talked to his mom, she had agreed to come to one of the meetings with him. Afterward, she'd hugged his neck, whispering, "I am *so* proud of you."

He wasn't done figuring things out. That would take a long time. But as he got in his car and sat there, thinking about all that had happened with Bree, he wondered if it was possible... With the baby...

He swallowed. A baby. *His* baby. His and Bree's. He was going to be a father, and yet he had managed to hold himself completely aloof from that reality as if he was peering through a window and coveting a life he could never have.

Except there were people who thought he could. People who had overcome bigger obstacles than his.

He thought about Bree's smile. That bewitching smile that he'd loved so very much. He remembered carrying her down that mountain and the reaction he'd had to her proximity. Her laughter. And making love on that balcony. Little by little, something had crept up on him. Something so quiet that he hadn't noticed it until it was far too late.

He loved her. And by God, he loved that baby. He just didn't know if he deserved either of them. If he could do right by either of them.

But other people had done it. They'd come out on the other side and had gotten their happy endings, despite the pain of their childhoods. Why couldn't he?

On that mountain, Bree had asked him how he would carry her down if he'd been bitten by that snake. It had been a light question. One that had made him laugh until he really thought about it. And he'd responded, "I would find a way."

Maybe he should start doing that. Start finding a way, before it was too late.

He swallowed. Maybe it already was. She'd been pretty upset when she left his office three weeks ago. But she had also said when he decided what he wanted to do to come and talk to her. So surely that meant that she'd left the door open.

At least, he hoped she had.

If not, he had to at least go and try. He couldn't make any black-and-white promises. But he could tell her he loved her and that he would do what he'd said: find a way. He could call her, but this wasn't a conversation he wanted to have over the phone. Or have at the hospital. He wanted to sit and look in her eyes and tell her exactly what he'd learned about himself. And exactly what his plan was to fix those areas that he didn't like.

He'd finally done the hard work that he'd told himself he was going to do and had approached this like a surgical plan. He'd gone in expecting to find that he was doomed and would be the worst thing possible for Bree or the baby. Had expected to be like that damaged mitral valve that he'd replaced in that pregnant woman during his and Bree's last surgery together. So far gone that it had to be surgically removed and discarded—replaced.

But he wasn't. And with the right counselor and a whole lot of blood, sweat and tears, he might just be able to make himself into a man his child—and Bree—could be proud of.

Starting his car, he headed to where she'd told him her new house was. It was about twenty minutes away. But when he pulled up in front of it, an eerie stillness washed over him. There was a For Sale sign in the yard out front. Shouldn't that be gone by now?

He got out, and as he headed up to the door, a woman with a notebook came out of the house, followed by a young couple who were probably in their mid- to late twenties. The woman held a child's hand, complaining about all the things they would need to fix if they bought this house.

The first woman eyed him. "Can I help you?"

"Wasn't this house already sold? I know the woman who was supposed to be buying it."

The man frowned and glared at the Realtor. "I thought you told us it was available."

"It is, I assure you. Can you excuse me for a minute?"

"Forget it," the man said. "We didn't like it anyway."

The couple skirted them and went through the open gate.

The woman planted her hands on her hips. "Okay. You have my attention. Now what is it that you want?"

"What happened to the woman who put a deposit down on this house? She showed me pictures of it."

"Are you talking about Signorina Frost?"

"Yes, did something happen?"

The woman's brows went up in a haughty way. "Yes, as a matter of fact, it did. She backed out at the last second. And I'll tell you, I didn't appreciate—"

Her voice droned on for several more sentences, but all he heard was that Bree had backed out of buying the house at the last minute. Backed out.

"Did she say why?"

A frown appeared on her face. "Like I said, she said she was going home to Naples and would no longer need it. Said I could keep the deposit. I told her I surely would."

Dios. There'd been something said about Naples some time ago, and he remembered how it had made him feel back then. Uneasy. Unsure.

Well, what he felt now was light-years from that lukewarm sentiment.

Desolation. Bleakness. Hopelessness.

Those were a few of the words that came to mind. And he didn't like any of them.

He'd avoided her like the plague at the hospital, and she must have done the same, because he hadn't caught sight of her in over two weeks. Maybe more.

"Did she say when she was going?" He held up a hand and looked back at the house. "Never mind. So since that couple evidently wasn't interested in the house, does that mean it's still on the market?"

Her demeanor changed in an instant, going from accusatory to saccharine sweet. She gave him a big smile and opened up her notebook. "Yes, it is, as a matter of fact. Do you want to take a look?"

He smiled and hoped to hell he was doing the right thing. "That won't be necessary. I've already seen it through someone else's eyes. Someone whose judgment I trust completely."

Bree finished packing the last of her belongings into suitcases. It was surprising how few things she'd bought since arriving in Catania. It was as if she'd somehow known she wouldn't be here all that long. Two months. And yet some pretty profound changes had happened in her life since her arrival.

And as much as she'd thought otherwise, she wouldn't change any of them. Because they had all helped her to grow and change and to learn what was truly important in life: this baby. Her life. And her family.

Something black and glittery caught her attention from under the foot of her bed. She frowned and bent to retrieve whatever it was.

The black flip-flops she'd bought on their race to the hospital. She brought them to her chest and hugged them tight. She hadn't had any problems throwing her other sandals away. But this pair?

"No. You're staying with me." They would be a reminder of a very magical time in her life. One that, despite the heartache it brought, she didn't want to forget.

She would still be in Catania for another month, or until the hospital could secure a new perfusionist, but she would be moving from this hotel to another, since the room was already booked for someone else. She was supposed to have been in her new house by now and had given the front desk a checkout date. She was lucky she'd been able to stay for an additional week until she could find a spot in another hotel.

She rang down and asked the front desk if they could call her a taxi.

"Actually, Signorina Frost, there's someone at the front desk to see you. Should I send him up? It's the gentleman you were with a few weeks ago."

Gentleman?

Her heart stuttered in her chest when she realized whom they were talking about. She should tell them to send him away. Tell him she was no longer interested in anything he had to say.

But she couldn't. It seemed like so long since she'd seen him. In reality, it was three weeks. Oh, she'd seen the back of his head once or twice. But the hospital was big enough that it had been easy to avoid each other.

But she wanted to see him. To talk to him. To share the same space with him. One more time.

And then she'd be free of him.

Liar. Well, lie or not, she wanted to hear what he had to say.

"Signorina?"

She realized she'd kept him waiting for longer than she should have. "Yes, please send him up. Thank you."

Hanging up, she glanced around the room. Her suitcases were strewn every which way, one on the couch, two on the floor. And those black shoes were still clutched in her hand. She carefully laid them on top of one of the bags on the floor.

She thought about trying to throw everything in a closet, but so what if he saw them? It was really none of his business where she went or when.

Had he heard that she was moving back home and coming to say his goodbyes?

God, she hoped not. Their last goodbye had been hard enough. To stand here while he muttered some platitudes and said she'd be missed would be excruciating.

She could always stand in front of the door and make him say whatever it was in the hallway, but she wasn't going to do that, either. He could come in and sit on the futon and be offered coffee and cookies. And she could drink in his presence one last time.

Once she left Catania, that was it. She would consider whatever this had been to be over.

A knock sounded on her door, but she barely heard it above the knocking of her heart. She suddenly felt breathless and faint and wondered if she would even make it through his visit without completely falling apart. But she had to. She did not want him to see how horrible these last three weeks had been. Wishing things could be different while knowing they would not be.

She opened the door, and there he was. The man she loved. The father of her child.

But he didn't sweep her off her feet or get down on one knee. Not that she'd thought he'd come for any of that. But still, it was like some remote part of her had still held on to a modicum of hope.

Sorry, hope. Not today. Maybe not ever.

"Come in."

He followed her into the room and glanced at the bags she'd packed. "So it's true."

She nodded. "Did they put that in the papers, too? Is it pinned on the bulletin board with a cute little picture?"

"No. I was surprised when I heard. And it wasn't from anyone at the hospital." He sat down beside her big suitcase and looked at her. "Why are you going?"

"Why not? My parents are still in Naples. They think I should be near them during the pregnancy. I tend to agree." Her initial impulse was to remain standing, but her knees were shaking so much she might as well sit before they rebelled completely and dumped her onto the floor.

"Bree, what if I asked you to stay?"

That modicum of hope grabbed the molecules around it and consumed them, growing a tad larger. But she and Diego been down this path before, and he'd wavered back and forth. She didn't know if she could bear going through that again. "Why would you do that?"

"Because I've come to the conclusion that I'm not beyond hope."

That simple phrase was not what Bree expected him to say. And her heart cramped into a small, hard lump that cried for him. Cried for whatever dark place inside him that had told him he was. She reached across the space and grabbed his hand and held on tight. "I know you're not. If I ever gave you that impression—"

"You didn't. You didn't need to. I've said it to myself almost my whole adult life. That having a real relationship was beyond my capacity. That having a baby was not even in the realm of possibility. So when you said you were pregnant… You have no idea." His fingers curled around hers. "I looked down at the ruined valve in that endocarditic heart, and it was like I was standing outside myself. I used my scalpel and carved it away—removed every trace of that part. A part that would only create death and destruction if it stayed. And in my head, I was carving away me."

The raw emotion in his voice was her undoing. She got up and climbed into his lap, held his head against her chest as words poured out of her that made little sense, only needing to reassure this man that he would not bring death or destruction. Not to her. Not to his baby. Not to himself.

"Look at me, Diego."

When he did, she said the words she should have said to him as soon as she discovered the truth. "I love you. I realized it a couple of weeks ago. I never wanted you to feel forced or trapped. It's why I gave my notice at the hospital."

He leaned up and kissed her. "You never made me feel trapped. I put myself into a cage years ago and locked the door behind me. I've met a group of people that have helped me search for the key. And I think I found it. I've been going to counseling. Learning how to deal with my past." He smiled. "And I'm learning how to plan for the future. A future I would very much like for you and the baby to be a part of. I love you, too. And I want you to know, I've renewed the vow I made on Etna. I will find a way to carry you down that mountain."

He was getting counseling? Oh God, that meant he was serious. Serious about being with her. Confident that they had a chance to make it, or he wouldn't be here, would he? "How about if neither of us carries the other? How about if we prop each other up when we're weak and encourage each other along when we feel we can't go on anymore."

His fingers threaded through her hair. "I think I can do that. With your help. Would you be willing to go to counseling with me? It might help us both."

"Yes." She would do whatever it took to have a chance to be with this man. To make their home on this island.

Home. Her brain froze.

"Oh, no!"

"What is it?"

"I let the contract go on the house I was looking at."

He frowned. "I know. I went over there to find you, but you weren't there, and the house is no longer on the market. And my place really isn't suitable for a baby."

"I wasn't expecting to move in with you. Not this soon. But I can't live in hotels forever. I'm already having to move from this one to another one because the room is reserved for someone else starting tomorrow."

"You might not have been expecting to move in, but I would very much like you to. I know it can't be today, but I'd like it to be sometime before the baby is born. You decide the when. But I already know the where."

"You do? But I thought you said your house isn't suitable."

"It's not. But I know one that is. It's the perfect house for you."

Hope surged inside her, growing to monstrous proportions. "It is? But how could you know that?"

"Because it's the one you picked out. The one you backed out on."

"But I thought you said it was no longer on the market."

"It's not, because I bought it. Before anyone else could."

Her head tilted, a smile coming to her face. "You bought *my* house?"

"I did."

She snuggled in closer. "I suppose you expect me to pay rent."

"No rent. But I would like us to design the nursery together. And I want us to pick out the baby's name. And I want us to make a life together. One that we'll both share in, equally."

It was too much. Her heart was set to burst in a million pieces, and she buried her face in his shoulder to keep him from seeing. But this kind of heartbreak was the good kind. Because those pieces would all knit back together, and in the cementing process, it would become stronger than it ever was before.

"I want that. All of it. And I want to live together sooner rather than later, once we work out all of the logistics."

She slid her hand beneath the sleeve of his shirt, where his tattoo lay hidden. "Don't you think it's time I hear the story of your dragon? You didn't want to tell me the last night we were together."

When he hesitated, she stopped him. "It's okay. It doesn't have to be now."

"No, it's okay. I want to. I got it as a reminder to myself that I can be hard to get along with. The hope was that I would temper myself. I'm not sure it worked."

"Hard to get along with. Really?" She nipped the side of his jaw. "I think your tattoo is very sexy. But I think you're more like a calamari—a lot more tender than one expects. And very delicious."

"Delicious, huh? I don't know about that." But his smile said he appreciated her words.

He placed his palm over her lower belly, filling her with a sense of wonder and love. She could trust him to stay. To work through his problems and to love her and the baby.

His words came back to her: he would find a way. But not just him. They both would. And if they couldn't *find* the way, they would forge a brand-new way. A path on which she, Diego and their children would journey. Together.

And that was enough.

EPILOGUE

A SLIGHT SOUND made Bree glance up from the ultrasound. She found Diego propped in the doorway of the clinic. "What are you doing here? I thought you had a surgery this afternoon."

"I asked Martini to step in and replace me."

Her eyes widened. "You did?" He had been true to his word and was working hard to make sure he made time for her and the baby. But she didn't want him to feel he had to cancel every surgery to do that. He had more than proved they had what it took to stick as a couple. And Diego had become a facilitator at the counseling center they'd both attended. They were doing a wonderful work and had given her new husband the courage he'd needed to break the cycle of his childhood. They'd forged that new path. And it was wild and crazy and filled with a truckload of happiness.

"I did." He came in and sat on the edge of the bed and toyed with a lock of her hair before looking at the image on the screen. "She looks like you."

Bree snorted and then laughed. "That's her behind."

He tilted his head and scrutinized the picture before ginning. "In that case, she looks like me."

This time the obstetrician gave a choked laugh, which she tried to cover with a cough. She reached over to the machine and pressed a button to print off an image. Of the face this time.

They'd found a clinic near their home in Catania, since it no longer mattered who knew about their relationship. In fact, they'd gotten married in the hospital chapel. It was a small intimate affair, nothing like the lavish wedding she'd planned with Sergio. She didn't need it. Didn't need the trappings. Didn't need hundreds of guests. All she needed were her parents, and Diego's mom and brother, and a handful of friends.

Teresina, the phlebotomist from Palermo, had stood with her as her bridesmaid. The two had become fast friends over the intervening months.

Bree looked at the obstetrician. "Is everything okay?"

"Yes. She's perfect. She is poised to come any day. But if you could have a little chat and ask her to come during daylight hours, I would appreciate it."

"Any? We still have a week to go before her due date."

"You're completely effaced and two fingers dilated. If I were a betting woman, I'd say you aren't going to make it another week."

"Dios!" Diego's face changed, the color draining from it.

"What is it?" Were the old fears coming back to haunt him again? If so, they could tackle them, just like they had with every other blip that had come their way.

"I haven't finished painting the nursery, and the crib is only—"

"Oh!" Bree blinked as something strange was released inside her. She reached over to grip Diego's hand. "I think it's too late to do any of those things."

"What? Why?"

"Because I think my water just broke."

The obstetrician looked from one to the other with a smile. "Too late? No, it's not too late. This is only the beginning. The start of a beautiful new life. For all three of you."

Diego reached down and kissed the top of Bree's head. "Yes, it truly is."

* * * * *

*If you enjoyed this story, check
out these other great reads from
Tina Beckett*

Their Reunion to Remember
Starting Over with the Single Dad
The Trouble with the Tempting Doc
How to Win the Surgeon's Heart

All available now!